AF243929

BIRDS OF APPETITE

A Novel by

Edward Lemond

Breachhousebooks

Barachois, New Brunswick

Cover artwork © Elaine Amyot
One Crow Sorrow

Lemond, Edward
Birds of Appetite

ISBN: 978-0-9780510-1-3

First paperback edition, 2011

Breachhousebooks
Chemin de la Brèche
Barachois, N.B., Canada

Printed in the United States of America
By www.lulu.com

For Alex and Anna

Where there is a lot of fuss about "spirituality," "enlightenment," or just "turning on," it is often because there are buzzards hovering around a corpse.

Zen and the Birds of Appetite – Thomas Merton

September 22 / Morning

You were up before dawn and went walking in the woods behind the monastery. All around as you climbed were the fallen trunks of rotting trees. Old Man's Beard, in tufts like wisps of tough, day-old cotton candy, clung to the shattered limbs where they lay. The air was cold – cold enough that you kept your hands deep in the pockets of the jacket. You could feel the way your shoulders swung left and right with each step and the ache from the old bursitis flared in the curve of the shoulders.

At the top of a small mountain with your back to the monastery you looked down at the wide, moon-lit bay. The moon was on the water, and it was in the tops of the trees, filtered through thin, white, floating layers of mist. Some quality of light and the dimensions of sky, trees, lake, and shoreline created an atmosphere that was warm and human and at the same time supernaturally clear.

You waited until you saw the moon dip low and touch the water with its light and you saw the stars and the heavens beyond the moon and you remembered the feeling of joy when you were in love just like it was yesterday. You remembered the day she came into your room at the hospital. You remembered the talks you had and the way you laughed together when she read you the comics. You remembered the way she touched you when she washed you and the words you kept saying to her over and over again, in thanksgiving. You remembered how terribly alone you felt the night she went away, and how you lay awake half the night, tormented by the knowledge that you were in love and that you did not want to live without her.

It was still dark when you came down out of the woods. I waited for you in the door of the chapel, thinking you were lost. You went in without a word. The chapel, on the ground floor of the east wing, under the bell tower, was cramped and vaulted as if in a basement. I moved off into the back row where I sat alone.

You stood five rows from the altar, eyes fixed on the shrivelled Corpus of birch wood set above the square, cloth-covered tabernacle. From the angle where I was sitting it looked like a jack-in-the-box. It was so quiet in the chapel I could hear the candles flickering, like miniature firecrackers going off.

I watched as you moved up, unhooked the rope, and walked forward to join the monks in the choir stalls.

No one objected to an outsider doing this. No one looked.

Many strong, deep voices rang out all around. I tried to guess which was yours. I let the voices wash over me, like waves wash over stones on a beach.

At six o'clock there was half an hour for private prayer and meditation before mass. Breakfast consisted of corn flakes, toast, milk and coffee. The coffee was bitter as ground slate. Everyone was quiet, not just because it was the rule. The quiet was something so real that you wanted to embrace it as you would embrace a lover.

After breakfast and after we had done the dishes we gathered in the library on the second floor. You talked about your travels and what you had seen since leaving Gethsemani. You let your mind wander back, and something in you opened like the water lily opens in sunlight. Your voice was sweet, musical, full of affection for the people you had met.

It seems incredible, you said, but just one week ago I was in New Mexico at an Apache encampment, taking part in secret ceremonies and dances marking the Feast of Tabernacles. I was with members of the Jicarilla tribe. What I liked most were the booths of boughs, tents and campfires everywhere, the wind blowing all the fires, then the coolness of dusk. The second day there were races, the young Apaches were racing to give back energy to the sun.

Father Raymond, the Abbot, was the first to speak up. Would you call them Christian, he wanted to know.

The way he looked at you, his eyes dark, round, and severe like the eyes of a hawk, suggested fireworks, but you rose to the challenge. Not the way you and I think of being Christian, you said, but it's hard to imagine a more spiritual people. The sun is the source of life and light, not a dying star in a dying universe. That's not Christian, but to my mind it's great. The clan that was fastest was the best painted and their first runner was like an African antelope with long yellow streamers flying from his head and a mirror in the centre of his forehead.

Father Raymond did not change his expression, but took in what you said and let it filter on down. A remarkable person, he had done his own share of traveling in his day. He was a French-speaking priest who got himself sent to India for 20 years and only came back because someone put a knife in his chest and punctured a lung.

Everyone rose. I followed you down the stairs to the main floor and into the gift shop. Brother Leo showed you where he kept your books where everyone could see them. You said you wanted to rest before we returned to town.

You waved to me and went down the hallway, through a door, and up three flights of stairs to the monks' quarters.

I walked along the road that led to the main highway that connected the mainland to the island. I stood there awhile enjoying the sight of the cars approaching, slowing at the entrance to the monastery, and moving on.

Circling back, I came down a pathway to a brook, and across a dam in the brook to a grotto. I climbed a hill above the grotto and followed a trail into the woods that bordered the lake that was formed by the dam across the brook.

I listened to the sounds of the birds in the woods, and the cracking of limbs.

By the time I returned to the main building you were waiting at the door, your small leather bag in your hand.

September 22 / Inside the Gazebo

Behind the house the hill sloped down to the edge of the cliff.

From the top of the cliff we looked out across the bay toward the little town that looked like no more than a few buildings nestled in among the dark spruce trees that stretched for miles all up and down the coast though in fact it numbered over ten thousand inhabitants.

The wind had died as if in answer to the dying of our conversation. A sailboat drifted idly toward the mouth of the bay. A shirtless man waved from the boat and called out, but his voice did not reach us, it was so far away.

The cliff was steep, fifty feet straight down, but when you looked out at a certain angle you felt you could almost touch the water, it seemed so close. Small dark birds, a dozen or more, flew toward the face of the cliff and disappeared, then others followed.

You moved closer to the edge, to see where they had gone.

The waves crashed on the shore below and swirled in among the rocks, the bands of dark green in the water marking the deeper, colder currents.

There is a kind of sparrow that builds its nest in the face of the cliff, I said. We'll go down to the beach later, if we have time, and I'll show you.

When we came to the small, ancient and wooden house I had made using wood from a collapsed barn, there was a procession of children holding up in their hands large mugs of hot coffee for their Father and his guest. I was beaming, struck that this was the first time in many weeks that I could say that I felt completely happy, completely at peace.

Behind the children came their mother with the dessert, a steaming apple strudel, dusted in white flour, on a long cutting board that had the shape of a cat's head.

Inside the gazebo was a round, white, plastic lawn table, big enough to seat eight, and through the screened-in windows we could see the sun falling across the bay and the grass on the hillside coming into shade.

Once everyone was settled she picked up the thread of the conversation that had only begun to take shape earlier, inside at the dinner table. What does it mean to be a monk in this day and age, she wanted to know.

She was agitated, as if she had a personal stake in the question.

I gave you a negative answer before, so I'll try and tell you what I really think. Being a monk today means being open to new ways, it means moving away from a strict authoritarianism. Let me tell you about a wonderful place that already exists in the desert in New Mexico. It's called Christ in the Desert. It's thirteen miles along a dirt road, in the middle of nowhere. It has three members and it's the finest monastery in America. There's a Navajo rug at the altar. The chapel is made of adobe and in constant need of repair. There are no fences to keep the prisoners inside. There's no need, the desert sees to that.

You thought it was time to shut up. You were talking too much. You were always talking too much, that's what they told you in Kentucky and you believed them.

We were all looking at you, waiting for you to go on. The sun dropped below the line of trees on the far shore of the bay. The clouds turned salmon red. The water in the bay, for one brief moment, was a white gold.

What about you, she said, what are you looking for?

Somewhere so remote there's no one around for miles and miles, you said. No one could care less if we have lay people, and women. It could be in New Mexico, Northern California, Alaska, or Nova Scotia.

I wouldn't like it in Alaska, Jason said. I hate it when it gets that cold.

How would you know when to get up if it's dark out all the time, Emma said.

For that matter how would you know when to go to bed, you said.

When you felt tired, Emma said.

But if it was still light at midnight I'd want to go out and play catch or something. I'd want to go out and look for polar bears.

Not me, Emma said.

I see a peaceful, remote mountain lake, a great expanse of water surrounded by mountains, and thousands of wild geese and ducks on the flats. I would build my cabin where I could look across the water to the tallest mountain.

The reception started early and you were late. You were feeling exhausted when you arrived, a little after seven, then you made the mistake of drinking a second glass of wine. Your head began to swim. You could not focus your thoughts, you kept forgetting people's names, in the end even your own.

From 'Brother Louis' you went to 'Louie' and then 'Satchmo.' Yes, you thought, I can live with that, to be Satchmo.

By nine o'clock you were almost dead. With a feeble apology you excused yourself and went upstairs. You stumbled down a dark hallway, past pictures of pretty girls doing the Highland fling.

Near the end of the hallway you entered a space far quieter and more sober. You stood there a moment, not wanting to move.

The window of your room looked down on the parking lot behind the motel. It was called the Claymore Inn. In the floodlight the cars glittered like dried, flattened codfish.

At the back of the lot was the dark woods. You remembered walking in the woods in Kentucky at night when you could not sleep and the trees were white with snow. You remembered throwing snowballs at the trees. You remembered the way the snow clung to the bark, making white blotches all up and down the bare trunk.

A pick-up truck, piled high with tables and chairs and a tattered mattress, passed along the highway above the Inn. You had seen it several times before, and it had entered into your consciousness like the memory of something very precious you had once seen as a child in the south of France.

You heard the bells on the mule without seeing anything.

Once, on a sunny, dusty day, the driver had on a green silk jacket, and a small red dog was running behind the wagon.

Another time, in a sheet of rain, the driver was riding bundled up in several old coats. The bells of the mule were ringing as if to call the dog home. The wagon was full to the point of bursting with baskets made of straw and stuffed full with old clothes. The green boards held themselves together miraculously, as if tied by an invisible rope.

As it passed behind the older of the two red-brick buildings the truck slowed almost to a standstill. The sign on the side said *Hadley Bros. Free Estimates.* In the distance, on the hillside above the hanging, swaying stoplight, was an illuminated sign, with the word *HOSPITAL* in large, green letters on a milk-white plastic background.

You felt the cool glass against your forehead and against the tip of your nose, and you recalled the words you whispered to the woman who came into your room at the hospital in Louisville, when you were almost asleep.

And I looked for you in the room where you worked but you were not there. I thought you were that patch of white moving quickly across the hallway to the door below the exit sign. I listened to the sound of scandal and the buzzer calling all doctors to the presence of alarm. I told you I'd meet you in some Kingdom I forgot and there the found would play the songs of the sent. A bird with all the shades of light would beat against your window and against my window. I would gladly consent to the kindness of strangers if only you did.

September 23 / Letter to Flavian

Antigonish

Sept. 23, '68

Dear Fr Flavian,

I'm writing this from the Director's Office at the Institute while waiting to get my flight to California confirmed. It is an unfamiliar typewriter so I don't guarantee the legibility of what I'm writing.

Also it is very good to be away from the typewriter for so long, with the prospect of being away from it still longer. The conference started last night with a reception and continued today with the first talk and panel discussions. I drank too much wine at the reception and my head aches - otherwise I'm fine. The people here are looking after me, making sure I get to where I want to go, and keeping me well fed. Archbishop Campbell is in Halifax, but I may meet him in a day or two. I believe he will be here for the last day of the conference.

I hope to do a lot more exploring in the next few days. There are tremendous areas here that are uninhabited, woods and lakes, mountains too, though not big mountains. People tell me that if I go across the channel to Cape Breton Island I will find many places of perfect solitude. Cape Breton Island is part of Nova Scotia but because it's an island and because it's very poor, it's a different world. It's not very far from where I'm staying.

Saturday night I slept over at the old Trappist monastery outside town. It belongs to the Augustinians now, but I could feel the spirit of those pioneer monks. The land here is not much good for crops, so you can imagine how hard it was those first few years. And they had fires and other catastrophes to contend with. We have things a little too easy by comparison.

The theme of the conference is the role of religion in the co-operative movement, which I'm sorry to say I know very little about. But I'm learning. There is a full program, with a two-hour talk every morning, followed by a discussion. After lunch there is a break from two until four, when the group sessions begin.

There are informal discussions and cultural events into the night.

The opening talk this morning was on the topic "Moses Coady and the Co-operative Movement." Moses Coady was known as the Man from Margaree. He was a priest, born in the Margaree Valley of Cape Breton Island. He was a leader in pushing for adult education and for the co-operative movement in the Atlantic Provinces. Compared to him I'm a late learner when it comes to the question of social justice.

For fifteen years in the monastery I cut myself off from these sorts of issues. I was very late in reading accounts of the Nazi death camps, as well as the atomic bomb attack on Japan. When I did finally came around to it, something in me shifted, like tectonic plates. A gap opened, and new material poured in. I discovered the poetry of Pablo Neruda, and friends in the publishing business introduced me to other poets, like Nicanor Parra.

A novice from Nicaragua, Ernesto Cardenal, gave me addresses of poetry magazines in Mexico, and I had an orgy of reading about South America. I read Octavio Paz, Cuadro, Andrada, and the poets of Brazil.

In August, 1957, I read Cardenal's poem attacking the United Fruit Company. I understood the connection that was being made between poverty and the exploitation of those who have no power and no say, and the violence that backs it up. I could begin to look back on my own life, especially the days in New York City in the 1930s and the work I did in Harlem in 1941, and I could see a direction not taken.

All my life I've felt a tension built on the twin themes of solitude and social concern. Most of this happened before you came on the scene, and I've never talked about it before. So maybe it's new and a little shocking but I don't think so. I think you know me well enough.

Best wishes to all,
Pray for me,
In the Lord,
Louie

September 23 / Swimming in a Sea of Goldenrod

You did not feel like lunch and made your way back to your room, to get away from the noise. You stretched out on the bed and tried to rest. A muscle in your face, below your right eye, would not stop twitching.

You closed your eyes and felt the pulsing not just in this one muscle, but in every part of your body. You lay still and let this deep consciousness form itself like a wave far out from shore that washes over you and through you. You lay quite still, the way a dragonfly will stay still for hours by the side of a pool, then suddenly vanish.

You changed clothes and stepped into the hall. You snuck out the back exit feeling that you must be doing something wrong but it was not clear what it was.

Antigonish reminded you of some of the little towns in upstate New York that you knew during your college days. Beneath the quiet, easy pace there was the feeling that things were happening. People were kind-hearted. If there were layers of social strata, which you knew there must be, it was very subtle.

You sat for an hour in a coffee house, listening to the soft, pleasant voices around you, reading the Halifax paper. On the wall there were paintings of sailing ships from a century ago. You felt at home in your blue jeans, blue denim shirt, and blue knit hat.

You decided to skip the group session in the afternoon and roam the town. You looked in all the windows on Main Street, and you wandered up the road to the campus.

There was a big barn of a church that you circled around, called St. Ninian's. You had no desire to go in.

In the basement of the Student Union was a bookstore with a good stock of high-priced text books, as well as a small selection of religious books including the new Tillich you had been wanting to read. After killing an hour in the bookstore, you went back down the hill, across the bridge, and along the road by the tracks.

You walked until you were in the country. It was so quiet and so beautiful to be looking across an open field that you stopped to breathe it in.

You walked more slowly now, at your leisure, and you did not look back. You forgot about time.

These fields were different from the ones you knew in Kentucky. They were flatter, and the grass was already brown. Only a few of the fields had been cut and harvested, most allowed to go wild.

In one field you sat cross-legged in high weeds. Everything around you was alive. You were swimming in a sea of goldenrod. You breathed slowly, in and out. The sky was blue, and the clouds white, like clusters of brand-new puffballs, perfectly round, with no scuffing, no discolouration.

You had no idea what time it was. Maybe it was late, maybe not.

You got up and started back into town. Darkness was falling, and you could see the lights in the buildings on the campus across the way, toward the top of a hill.

You were glad you had escaped the hothouse atmosphere of the conference, if only for a while. You wondered what they were saying about you because you were not there. Had they sent someone to search for you?

But you did not really care.

September 24 / The Monk and the Marxist

In the front row sat a black cleric with a tag that said that he was from Ghana and a smile that said, What have you got to say that is relevant to me?

You liked the fact that you were not talking to the same old tired white faces.

When he looked at you, it was with an expression that was both expectant and accusing.

You put aside the paper that you had written and began to talk informally.

It feels strange, wearing this monk's robe because I never, never wear this robe. The question I want to address is, Who do I represent, what am I doing here, what does the life of a monk have to do with the life of any person, man or woman, engaged in concrete action. A monk is a very strange kind of person, a marginal person, who withdraws deliberately to the margin of society with a view to deepening fundamental human experience. The monk is essentially someone who takes up a critical attitude toward the world and its structures. The monk is somebody who says, in one way or another, that the claims of the world are fraudulent.

A man with a camera moved in. You held your hands up instinctively, the right hand higher, protecting your eyes.

Now this is a dreadful thing to say, especially now that it's being said on TV, but the point I'm trying to make is that there has to be a dialectic between world refusal and world acceptance. The world refusal of the monk is something that also looks toward the acceptance of a world that is open to change. In other words the monk is like the Marxist, except that the Marxist talks about changing substructures, while the monk is seeking to change consciousness. I think it's important that we acknowledge the similarity. I won't say anything more about Marxism today, because I'm writing a paper on the subject that I'm going to give later when I get to Asia. Anyway I've probably offended enough people already. Monasticism starts from the problem inside man himself. Instead of dealing with the external structures of society monasticism starts with man's own consciousness. Monasticism says that the root of all the problems that plague us is that man's consciousness is all fouled up and he does not apprehend reality as it really is. The moment he looks at something, he begins to interpret it in ways that are prejudiced and predetermined to fit a certain wrong picture of the world, in which he exists as an individual ego at the very centre of things. What I'm saying is that from the perspective of monasticism you can't change the world in any important way without first changing human consciousness. I think the cooperative movement recognizes this at some level because of the emphasis on adult education. Education raises the level of consciousness. We can't all be monks, but we can all be hungry for knowledge. Maybe there's no deeper desire in the human soul than the desire to know. If that's heresy, so be it. The point is that monasticism shows one way to change human consciousness, and adult education shows another. What I'm saying is, first change consciousness, then change the world.

On that note you ended your talk. The camera came in even closer. The light was in your eyes, and you could not see the people in the audience. The moderator came forward and stood next to you. While applause filled the hall he turned and whispered something in your ear.

Did you want to take questions?

You shook your head. No.

I believe the plan is to break now, the moderator explained, and those who want will reconvene in the chapel to hear Mass. The real debate will have to wait till later this afternoon.

You nodded agreement.

But when you turned to leave the stage you staggered and almost fell.

Several people rushed forward to assist.

Augury of what was to come.

September 24 / Into the Woods

For the second day in a row you skipped lunch. You were not hungry, and the last thing you wanted to do was continue this sort of abstract conversation around the dinner table. You did not like yourself when you talked this way. You felt like a cheap toy. As if someone had come up behind you and wound you up and sent you on your way, blabbering and jabbering.

You took a shower and lay down to rest.

Two other participants in the conference stopped in the hallway just outside your door, talking and arguing. One voice you recognized as belonging to a 65-year-old priest from Montreal who had spent the last twenty years of his life among the poor of Haiti.

He was passionate on the subject of Marxism and existentialism. You had talked with him briefly before the opening session, and when you said something about Marxism that was only mildly positive, he jumped all over you. From what you could hear through the door the old priest was continuing the same line of argument.

More harangue than argument, it was a critique of Marxism and the seductive power of Marxism, but this time he was drawing his ammunition from a different source, not Camus, the existentialist, but Marcuse, the political theorist.

All highly organized societies, he said, all so-called managerial societies end up by being equally. ...

The voices trailed off as the two men moved on down the hallway. You stood in the door and looked outside, to see if they were gone. There was fire in the old priest's talk, but you wanted more than fire. You wanted to go very deep, go where it was dangerous, where there was more water than fire, more dirt than fresh air.

There was something so innocent about the people, you found it sad. Something was troubling you, something in you was unborn, but you were not ready to look at it.

Downtown you ducked into a newsstand and spent half an hour in the back, looking through the weekly news magazines.

The news was depressing, the ads even more so. Everybody wanted what they didn't have, seemed to be the message. And that's just fine, was the underlying message.

You walked along Main Street, on the cracked sidewalk. When the sidewalk ended you kept to the dirt shoulder at the side of the road. You followed the road away from the railroad tracks, inland, into low rolling hills.

It was a busy road, with cars and trucks speeding by. Whoosh.

You walked on the right side of the road, with your back to the traffic, though you knew better. You did not care if it was dangerous. If a car swerved and hit you, what did it matter?

About a mile outside of town you left the road and cut across a field to some woods. You hungered for woods. In woods you could breathe better. Your thinking became calm and settled.

You walked on, away from the road and the sound of the trucks and the cars. The only sound was the leaves and the twigs underneath your feet when you stepped on them.

If you stopped and listened there was only silence. If you stopped long enough without moving you could hear birds in the distant trees.

At the bottom of a hill you were surprised to find a stream running through, four or five feet across, two or three feet deep, clear enough to see stones on the bottom. You stopped a moment and listened to the sound of the water.

It was cool by the water. You pulled your shirt tight around your shoulders. A shudder ran through you like a train runs through a tunnel.

Do not move. Listen to the silence.

Five minutes passed. Ten minutes. You lost track.

The sound of the water flowing underfoot was delicious. You took slow, deep breaths of air, swallowing them like quaffs of water. The upper part of your body heaved with the air filling and leaving the lungs.

You were waiting for something. It was close by, you knew. You could hear it move in the woods across the brook. You could feel it scramble through the leaves and twigs.

But when you opened your eyes and looked, the sound stopped.

Whatever it was, it was not here. It was somewhere else.

You walked up the hill, and along the road into town.

September 24 / Supper

Many of the stores were already closed for the day. Where had everyone gone?

On the sidewalk by the bookstore were boxes of books on a long folding table that looked so wobbly, so feeble you wondered how it was still standing. Near the curb was a sign made of wood, two pieces hinged together with a chain at the bottom, light enough that it would blow away in a big wind. On the flimsy vinyl pasted to the wood were printed the words Buy – Sell – Trade.

She opened the door, surprised to see you. You smiled your enigmatic smile, lips glued tight in a round face. You offered to help her bring everything in.

She had several tasks inside the store to run through – a radio to be turned off, a teapot to be rinsed out, a pocketful of petty cash to be hidden inside a hollowed out book, credit notes to be filed, lights to be turned off. You had not imagined it could get this involved.

You waited on the sidewalk while she locked up.

The sun was low in the sky. The houses on the hills above the downtown and the woods beyond the houses grew dark in outline.

She walked you around the building to where the car was parked. She did not know what you wanted, or why you were here. You did not know yourself.

If she did not say anything, you would go back to the motel where you were staying and that would be that. You did not want to push anything.

She asked you to come to supper because she knew you would say yes. The kids would love to see you again.

Without thinking you accepted. Nobody was more surprised than you.

In the car on the way out of town you talked about the weather, about her day at the store, about your talk that morning at the Institute, about everything and anything except what was really on your mind.

Climbing the hill above St. George's Bay, you watched the sun set and turn a deep red. It was huge, like the appetite for love growing in you.

The town was behind you. The water was far below, passing in and out of view. You were surrounded on every side by the trees and the falling dark.

You felt tired, and realized how much you wanted to fall asleep against her shoulder with her arms around you.

She must never know.

Arriving at the house and seeing the children made you happy. Entering into the noisy give-and-take of the family as we sat down to supper together brought you to life.

I'd heated a seafood chowder, with crabmeat, pieces of lobster, and a white fish that could have been cod. Sprinkles of tarragon on top.

Little Emma, who liked to stir things up, said that the tarragon looked like the wings of an insect that had been broken into bits.

Some cultures eat insects, you said between spoonfuls. It can be a great delicacy.

These are fly wings, Emma said. Do people eat flies?

I don't know about flies but they eat locusts, you said, playing along. And termites. And grubs.

Nobody's hungry enough to eat grubs, Jason said, wincing at the word *grubs* as if he had just swallowed one.

In Kentucky, where I live, they make a delicious stew with carrots and turnips and big fat tasty grubs. Right, Emma?

Right. Sure.

And I bet they mix in spiders too, Jason scowled.

Sometimes they do, you said.

I saw a show on TV the other day, she said in a voice that made it clear she thought it was time for some grown-up talk. It was about a tribe of Indians that lives in South America in the forests of the Amazon. They're called the Yano-mani, or Yano-nami, something like that. Anyway they have the most amazing diet, including wild animals like pigs, turkeys, armadillos, anteaters, and monkeys. They have big gardens where they cultivate many kinds of vegetables and fruits. They have their little delicacies, including grubs, caterpillars, and roasted spiders. They seem very healthy and happy.

The noble savage, I said beginning to clear away the soup bowls. I saw that show too, and what I saw wasn't so noble. There was a lot of wife beating to start with. Apparently that's the approved method of proving your manhood. Family planning consists of infanticide. If a woman becomes pregnant while she's still nursing her last child, she will kill the new baby so as not to deprive the older child of milk.

I'm not exactly in favour of wife beating, she said. But I don't think we should impose our ideas on other cultures. Look at what we're doing in Vietnam.

Vietnam is not about the clash of cultures, it's about the clash of ideologies.

We go over there to 'liberate' the Vietnamese, and what happens, we end up destroying them. We don't respect them. We don't understand them. We don't even want to understand them. The only thing we know is they're commies.

She was in full flight, there was nothing stopping her. It was Billy Graham the other day who said that the war we're fighting now is a spiritual war between good and evil. I think that's a very dangerous way of thinking because it sanctions all kinds of horrors.

If you can't be fair, I said, at least try to be balanced.

I don't know what balanced means, she said.

I read somewhere a very sad comment by a Catholic Youth leader in Saigon, you said. Many people had told him not to trust Americans, but he had never accepted it until now. He had believed the Americans were there to help his people, but they were destroying everything and he hated them for it.

That was the point I was trying to make, I said.

You still don't get it, she said.

Maybe not, I remain to be enlightened, fire away.

I'm afraid we're boring Tom half to death.

Not at all, though I must admit I feel a little talked out myself

What about that, I said. As a Trappist you take a vow of silence. So how does that work, when you travel outside the monastery?

I also took a vow of stability, which means you don't travel outside the monastery. But as you can see, here I am.

Good thing too, she said.

We fell silent. The children excused themselves and ran off to play. You finished your second glass of wine. She disappeared into the kitchen with the dinner plates.

What was on the agenda for tomorrow, you wanted to know.

In the morning there's a talk on the idea of poverty. I forget who's speaking. In the afternoon there's the usual group session.

The thought of more of the same sort of talk made you feel listless. You were pale as a ghost. I don't think I'm all that interested, you said. I'm afraid that could be seen as ungracious, after all the trouble the organizers took to invite me. The truth of the matter is I'm feeling a bit tired.

I said how sorry I was to hear it.

You said that what you really wanted was to do some traveling and see what the country was like. From all reports Cape Breton was the sort of place where you'd like to spend some time. It could be the place you were looking for, where you could set up a permanent colony of like-minded monks and lay people.

It's very beautiful, I said.

I've got nothing against beauty, you said, but what's important is wildness.

There's plenty of wildness but maybe it's not real wildness. If you want real wildness, then you have to go north, into Newfoundland, or Labrador, or northern Quebec.

Since Newfoundland and Labrador and northern Quebec were out of the question you said you'd settle for Cape Breton. I'll take off for a couple of days. No one will miss me.

I'm not so sure, I said.

What about it? Do you want to come along?

I said I wasn't free because I was teaching the next day, and the day after that.

What about cancelling classes?

I don't think that's possible.

Anything's possible.

At this point she came back in, with a tray with the pot of tea, three cups, and a little bowl of honey with a spoon. I happened to overhear what you were saying, she said. I could drive.

What about the bookstore?

I can find someone to look after the bookstore.

And the children?

He can take care of the children, she meant me. He has a healthy maternal instinct. He always did. The children will be fine.

I don't want to cause any problems.

There's no problem, I said.

There, it's settled, she said.

You felt much better already. Just the thought of being on the road was like a shot in the arm – not that you had ever had a shot in the arm, or a shot in the leg, or a shot anywhere, not that I know of.

September 25 / Cape Breton Island

At Margaree Forks the road turned to the north to follow the river to the sea. The hills became higher and more interesting in the way they suggested distance and quiet. The fall colours, under a sky of broken, grey-white clouds, had a bright, metallic finish.

For a long while you sat quietly on your side of the car, looking out the window and feeling content, in a sort of swoon, a sort of ecstasy, with half open eyes, taking everything in.

She talked about the time she traveled in Europe, her memory of crossing the mountains from Austria into Italy. She loved the high mountains, the gorgeous, warm sun, but more than anything she loved the people. They seemed to live more intensely than in Austria.

She remembered stopping at a look-off as she came down out of the mountains and shouting across the valley for sheer joy. I feel the same way whenever I cross the causeway to Cape Breton Island, she said.

She remembered going whale watching once at the northern tip of the island, near a place called Meat Cove. The captain of the boat said that the people in the houses still spoke Gaelic. Beyond Meat Cove was the last really wild part of Nova Scotia. There were no roads. Nothing but unbroken woods, rocky beach, and the cold Atlantic ocean.

I'd like to go there, you said, if you'll take me.

But if it's too far, too wild, too windy, too wet, too cold, too steep, too slippery, too dangerous, too anything, you wanted her to say so.

But you already knew the answer that she would give. She was willing to go anywhere you wanted, that was the scary thing. Because the one thing that you knew for sure was that often you did not know your own mind.

You closed your eyes, and you let the countryside roll by. Before you saw the ocean you could smell it, and when you came down the hill toward the coast the water was blue.

Where the sun glinted it was white.

You were traveling to some place as remote as you could get, and she was your guide. This, you thought, was practice for the real thing – the Himalayas.

In a month you planned to be there. The thought took your breath away.

She talked about stopping somewhere for lunch at a place that was known for its seafood. In answer to her question you said that you didn't know if you liked seafood because you did not eat seafood at Gethsemani.

It's probably against the rules. Or maybe not. No one tells me what the rules are.

I'd hate to be your downfall, she said.

Something in the way you looked at her made her laugh.

She tried to imagine what you'd be like as a lover.

You put a finger to your lips, as if to seal them. There was a ribbon of warm blood that wound its way up from your shoulders through the back of the neck right up to the top of the head.

You liked this place, now that you were here. You could understand Moses Coady the dreamer of dreams. Everyone seems to feel everyone else's pain.

Part of the reason for that is it's an island, she said.

Everyone's in it together, you said.

Yes, she said, but at the same time it's big enough a person could get lost if he wanted to.

Good, that's why I'm here, you said, to get lost. That, before anything else.

The restaurant was called the Duck Cove Inn. The menu included seafood chowder, fried clams, and baked salmon. Through the window you could see the river flowing under the flat bridge into the sea, emptying itself, leaving banks of gravel that glistened like wet chalk.

A sea gull, as white as milk, took ginger steps along the narrow beach, next to where the river ran into the sea. You had never seen a gull so white, or so big.

A second gull came and settled next to the first. There was something otherworldly about them. They came and went and no one knew where they came from or where they went to. There was a lesson in that, if you only knew what it was.

The bowl of chowder and the slice of homemade bread were for her. The plate of deep-fried clams and French fries was for you. The waitress wanted to know where you were from.

When you told her that you were from Kentucky, she said she would never have guessed it from the accent.

We don't get that strong southern accent you're thinking about, you explained.

She looked away, as if slapped. You folks enjoy your lunch now.

The chowder was too hot. She set her spoon down. I had an interesting dream last night, she said.

You shifted in your chair. Leave me out of your dreams, you wanted to shout, but you held your tongue.

It was not your first mistake with her but your first big mistake.

What kind of dream, you said.

It seemed ordinary enough in the beginning, she said. I was walking home from work, feeling tired and not looking forward to seeing anyone. I turned the corner on my block and saw a man standing there on the sidewalk in front of my house. I watched as he went up to the house and looked through the window. He wore a robe with a hood drawn up over the head. I was afraid.

I don't blame you, you said.

I don't usually remember colours in my dreams but this time I did. It was a dark brown like the brown of the lamp by the side of my bed. I came closer, but when I saw that it was you, Thomas Merton, the famous monk, I was no longer afraid. I was happy and I ran to you and we embraced. I felt surrounded by light. Is this what you mean by infused light, I asked.

I suppose I was fool enough to answer, you said.

For an answer you held your finger to your lips, the way you did just a minute ago. The next thing I know it's no longer you I'm holding, but the Buddha. I wake up terrified.

Why terrified?

Because of the expression on his face. I once saw a picture of a bronze statue of the Buddha that was described as weighing two hundred thousand pounds. The weight did not frighten me, but the face did. The features were round and sensual, but the expression cold and haughty. The Buddha in my dream had this very same look.

This was a false Buddha, you said. The real Buddha is detached from things but not cold, not haughty. The real Buddha is full of compassion but it's a detached sort of compassion. I know I'm preaching here but it's what I think.

I don't understand this detachment business, she said. I'm looking for what connects me to people.

I feel connected with people but I don't go looking for it, you said.

That's where we're different, she said.

You won't find it if you're looking for it, you said.

She was not convinced but said nothing more.

You watched the seagulls through the smudged window.

After a while the gulls were joined by a half dozen small shorebirds that moved back and forth over the sand with such fast little legs that when you and she looked at each other you both burst out laughing.

September 25 / The Stunted Woods

Inside the National Park there were no towns, no houses, no service stations. After two hours in the car she felt like stretching her legs, and so did you. At the next side-road she turned in.

The road became a path. The path crossed bog and Balsam Fir habitat to a hilltop that rose a hundred feet above the sea. Because of the wind coming across the water fiercely year after year, the trees were stunted, in what a sign at the entrance to the trail described as the *Krummholz Effect*.

You had never seen anything like this before.

It was as if you were in a miniature forest, in a fairyland, or an amusement park. But here you were, and it was real.

She went ahead, stopped and waited for you, then went ahead again. You saw how young she looked when she was fired up. You admired her, the easy way she breathed, her trim, small-breasted body, her long legs.

She could outpace you any day even if she was the same age as you. At most, she was a few years younger.

In places where the path was muddy you could see the way her walking shoes were getting caked, and the cuffs of her jeans splattered. But she did not care and kept pushing on, leaving you farther and farther behind.

Fifty feet from the end of the trail, among the stunted trees, she heard a noise that caught her attention. A tree branch snapped.

A full five seconds she stared into the woods before she saw what had been there all along – a moose, perhaps no more than a year or two old, too confused to know where he was or where he wanted to go.

You stood behind her where you could feel her touching your chest when she leaned back into you. He's huge, you whispered in her ear.

He's not even fully grown, she said.

Will he charge?

Moose are shy creatures, more afraid of us than we are of them.

Without taking its deep, brown, pinhole eyes off her, the moose defecated. In the next second it had turned and vanished with two spring-like steps into the cropped, mountain woods.

Just like that, gone, you marvelled.

Whoosh.

That's how I would like to disappear one day, lightning fast, like a moose.

Beyond the trail was a long loping hillside covered in grass and reaching to the top of the cliff. Beyond the cliff lay the immensity of ocean and sky.

There was the feeling that you could just float off into this immensity and be safe.

With her eyes she followed the coastline where it twisted and looped below in a line that stretched far into the distance. Once again you found yourself standing near, almost touching her shoulder.

She turned to you and said, Do you think I'm crazy because I had a dream about a two hundred thousand pound Buddha.

Not at all.

You seem to be scared of me. You never ask me what I'm thinking or anything.

You never come close except to tease.

I'm sorry if that's how I come across.

You wanted to take her into your arms and hold her but you were afraid.

I feel lost when I'm with you, she said.

Look at the ocean, you wanted to tell her, it's green one moment, blue the next. Far out it touches the sky. In close it washes the stones on the beach. In such a world we're all lost. There's something very sweet in that.

The spray on the rocks below was like a fine mist from this height.

What if something makes her want to jump? What can I do?

It has nothing to do with me.

You wanted to tell her not to tempt fate. Nature will always win out. The wheel of life and death, there's the primary contract.

But what you hated more than anything was preaching, and so you kept your mouth shut.

Below you a great black-backed gull floated by, wings steady, gaze fixed, almost brooding. It wheeled past where you and she were standing near the cliff's edge, then turned and flew out over the water.

Slowly at first, with an effort that seemed monumental, then more rapidly and gracefully, the bird began beating its heavy wings. It knew exactly where it was going, you thought, yet there was nothing out there but sea and more sea.

She scanned the horizon, holding her hand up as a shield from the sun. A boat appeared on the horizon, where sea and sky merged.

Come away from the cliff, you said.

She gave you her hand, and you led her away from the cliff, away from the danger.

Like the blind leading the blind you found your way back again into the stunted woods, along the pathway through the woods to the gate, and through the gate into the parking lot.

September 26 / Before Dawn

You stopped for the night at a bed and breakfast outside the town of Bay St. Lawrence, on a hill overlooking the Atlantic Ocean. She was tired after the long drive and went to bed early.

You read awhile and fell asleep with your book tented on your chest. You slept soundly until four, got up, read a psalm, wrote down what you remembered of a dream (in the dream you lost all your teeth), dressed and went outside.

It was dark. The quiet was deeper and darker than any you had experienced. You had never been this far north, in a land with so few people and so few lights.

You walked along the highway toward the little town, wishing you had a scarf to tie around your neck, under the jacket, to keep out the cold. High hills surrounded you, as dark and threatening as storm clouds. Above the hills the sky was clear and black, with hundreds, thousands of bright stars.

The harbour at Bay St. Lawrence was sheltered on four sides, with a narrow outlet to the sea between two high walls of reinforced concrete. You found a place where you could stretch out flat on your back, and you spent the next hour looking up at the stars.

Cassiopeia, in the shape of a W, was straight overhead. Once you had Cassiopeia it was easy to find Perseus, then Andromeda.

With a slow, deep movement of your lungs and chest, you breathed in the cold, crisp, salt air. You had the feeling that you could remain here forever.

The stars like words that go on forever.

September 26 / Thoughts of a Night Traveler

The world is my cell, any hut in the forest will do, physical solitude above all, do nothing to gain the public eye, the hermit wants one thing only, contemplative union with God, not silence alone, not meditation alone, but meditation in the silence of the woods, leading to perfect contemplation, silence of the tongue, silence of the body, silence of the heart, no useless and evil speaking, no useless and harmful action, no useless and evil thought, silence builds the life of prayer, silence, prayer, opening to God, sense of oneness with the universe, is that heretical, deep, interior prayer, the mind at rest, infinite compassion, hence the attraction of Buddhism.

September 26 / Nude Descending

With the coming of dawn to Bay St. Lawrence you rose from your makeshift bed and made your way up the road from the wharf to the highway. There were lights on now in some of the houses.

As you went along the highway to the bed and breakfast fog gathered below you in the black harbour. A pick-up truck passed you on the way to the wharf. The sky was grey and remote. Gulls called from somewhere beyond the lighthouse.

Your arms and shoulders began to shake with the cold.

In the antique kitchen you warmed your hands in the steam of the electric kettle. The cup of instant coffee, as bitter as any you had tasted, heated your insides.

As you climbed the stairs to your room, you heard a noise – the sound of a door being opened or closed.

You looked up.

She appeared in a red and white spotted nightshirt that was so short that it gave you an unobstructed view of her sex.

The way you bent your head looking up at her shut off the flow of blood into the brain, and you came very close to fainting and falling back down the stairs.

Or maybe it was that you had not seen a woman in thirty years.

You felt yourself plunging headfirst toward a new sort of catastrophe.

As you came closer she said very softly, so as not to wake the other guests, You've probably been up half the night.

Since four to be exact, you said.

You were standing two steps below her, which had the advantage that you were looking at her face not her sex, the disadvantage that you were close enough to feel the heat of her body and smell her perfume.

So this is what it's like, you said to yourself. I had forgot, maybe I never knew. All these years going without. What a shame.

You had gone down to the wharf to view the stars you told her. They were fantastic stars, more than you had ever seen, opening into more distant places.

She had been awake since five. She couldn't sleep and finally got up and read awhile. When she looked out the window it was grey as ash, so thick she couldn't see the road. She had a bad headache, the worst one she could remember.

You said you were sorry to hear that.

She asked if you would come and keep her company.

I don't want to offer you something I can't deliver on, you said.

I'm not asking you to sleep with me. That's out of the question, I know that.

How does she know that, you asked yourself.

Just so there's no confusion, you said.

She wanted you to put your hand on her head. That's all. That's not asking much.

You followed her into her room. The fog seemed to have followed you back, rolling with you on up into the house, on up the stairs to where you were standing, on up into your brain so that your memory and all your powers of thinking were impaired.

You placed your hand, which still had the memory of the cold of the early morning stars, on her forehead. That's where it hurt the most, she said.

Words are like that. They deceive, and pile up. They do not know where they want to go, and then, because of two or three or four that suddenly come out, simple in themselves – a personal pronoun, an adverb, a verb, an adjective – there's the excitement of seeing them come to the surface through the skin and the eyes.

Sometimes the nerves cannot bear it any longer. They put up with a great deal. They put up with everything. It is as if they were wearing armour as protection from the onslaught, but to no avail.

September 26 / Letter to Flavian

Bay St. Lawrence

Dear Fr Flavian,

I'm in a little room in a house that belongs to a family with a French name - Comeau.   They call this sort of thing a bed and breakfast. I've just had the bed and in a little while I'll go down and try the breakfast. The people here are very friendly.

Whatever else I may say - it is clear that I like Nova Scotia much better than Kentucky and it seems to me that if I am to be a hermit in North America, Nova Scotia is probably the place for it. Bay St. Lawrence is at the northern tip of Cape Breton Island, which is technically part of Nova Scotia - But really very different.

I'm driving around the island looking for a place where there's enough solitude for a hermitage. The man who's supposed to be driving me could not find the time, so his wife volunteered - a very nice woman who owns a bookstore and teaches Yoga and practices how to seduce lonely monks. I'm just joking - Never fear.

It was Oscar Wilde who said, I can resist everything except temptation. Evidently, I am not very different from Oscar Wilde in this regard. I suppose that just means I am human, like everyone else. You know what happened two years ago, at the hospital in Louisville - I don't need to remind you of that painful episode, which is now behind us - Thank God. I learned then how very human I am. It was a lesson I needed to learn - But I do not need to learn it again.

Heraclitus said, The soul determines its own fate. I believe I'm moving toward something that might be called my fate - And this has nothing to do with what anyone else might want to dream up for me. This is the conviction that I hold fast to at any rate, while all around me the great big sea heaves and storms.

Pray for me,
Warmest regards,
Louie

When I entered the monastery, in December, 1941, I expected that I would never see the outside world again. The vow of stability meant that I would live and die and be buried inside the enclosure. The only possible exception would be for reasons of personal health. I would not attend the burial of family or friends. I would not go anywhere for pleasure or personal gain.

For seven years I went outside the strict enclosure only to work in the monastery grounds. In August, 1948 I traveled to Louisville for six hours on business for the Order. In the next ten years, aside from visits to hospitals, I made only four trips outside the monastery, two to Louisville to become an American citizen, one to Ohio to look at a site for a new foundation, and one to Minnesota to attend a conference.

Toward the end of the 50s the winds of change were sweeping across the land - And they reached even into the monasteries. Freedom was in the air, anything seemed possible, and my requests for travel met with approval more and more frequently.

Around this same time I felt my spirit growing more rebellious. I no longer tried to hide it. There were occasions when I left the enclosure without permission, to spend a few hours with friends, walking in the woods, taking photographs, sitting on a blanket in the grass, having a picnic, drinking a bottle of wine. Sometimes I was gone the whole day.

The crisis came two years ago, in 1966, when I fell in love. I suppose it was inevitable, given all the other rules I had been breaking for the better part of a decade. She was a student nurse at a hospital in Louisville. She had black hair that she kept tucked under her cap, large grey eyes, pale skin, an oval face. She washed me after the operation and helped me to dress. She told me her name. I loved saying her name. I said it over and over, and she laughed.

In all my letters and in my journals I've always called her S. - to protect her anonymity. I did so little else to protect her.

For several months we exchanged letters, talked by telephone, arranged secret meetings in Louisville and right outside the monastery grounds. I felt emotions that I had thought were impossible for me to feel again. I considered leaving the monastery and getting married. I was very close to a decision that would have changed everything forever. Left to my own devices, I could have gone either way. But then they found out about us - Somebody was listening to our phone calls. I was called to account. The biggest shock was to hear my name bandied about - and hers.

Come to your senses, man - that's what they all said. They tried to make me see how dangerously I was living, how foolish my dreams were, how much pain I was causing my superiors, my friends, and everyone - especially the woman.

All during the years before I met her I had been searching, inside and outside the monastery, for a place of more perfect solitude. Very often I felt trapped in the everyday life of a monk. I wanted my own cabin in the woods, outside the strict enclosure. There was a long running battle with one superior after another on this subject of a hermitage. It was so bad that once, ten years ago, they brought in a well-known psychiatrist who labelled my "hermit trend" pathological - Complete humiliation. But I did not give up, and finally I got what I wanted, a cabin in the woods where I could be alone just as I dreamed.

I was able to live the life of a hermit, with very few obligations to the community. I could keep the hours I wanted and do the writing that was in me to do. Books and letters, poems and pamphlets poured from my pen, in a great burst of energy. Even at the hermitage, though, I did not find the peace that I craved, and this began to disturb me and cause me to worry about my own sanity. The quiet I desired was often broken by visitors – friends and strangers alike. The great publicity machine was at work, and there was no stopping it - It was depressing.

I promised I would never talk about her, so if I write this down it's strictly for private consumption. Even for this I beg her forgiveness. It seems important to get it down and be clear in my mind. She was from Cincinnati, but she could have been from anywhere. There was nothing distinctive about her - at first sight. The first thing I thought about her, when she came into my room at the hospital, was: She's starved for talk. She wanted to talk about the new liturgy. Then she wanted to talk about one of my books she had read. She told me that her father was an artist and enjoyed solitary walks. She told me that she liked Mad Magazine, and we talked about that for a while. Just before she left, she tidied up the room, doing her best to show that she was in charge. For once I agreed to follow orders, much as I hate following orders.

I did not see her over the weekend, and I thought she had been transferred to another ward. When she came into the room Monday morning, she said she had had a cold. I felt so elated seeing her that I didn't know what to say. I stumbled over my words. We laughed out loud remembering things in Mad Magazine.

On Wednesday night she came to my room to say goodbye. She was leaving for Chicago to see her fiancé. For the first time she was in a dress, and her hair was free. I felt as light as air. I asked her to write her address in my notebook so I could send her things I had written. She asked if she could come out some Sunday to the monastery to see me. I said this was impossible. We said goodbye, and she went off in the rain for the airport. I lay awake half the night, trying to hear the sound of an airplane. My world was turned upside down. I realized I was in love and I did not want to live without her.

She was starved for talk. I was starved for love. I wrote a letter for her to find when she came back from Chicago, saying I needed friendship. I called it friendship, because I still did not want to admit it was love. I don't think she was fooled for one minute. I had spent twenty years turning myself into something like a human being, and now here I was, this was the real thing, no more playacting. It was painful.

At the monastery I pretended that nothing had changed. I told myself I needed solitude and nothing else. This went on for a week - until I got her first letter. I wrote a declaration of love and sent it out under

'Conscience Matter.' Without waiting for her reply, I phoned her and we agreed to meet when I came back into Louisville for a post-op check, in a couple days.

I think I went a little crazy then, for about two months. One time I invited her to the monastery for a picnic. She brought a bottle of wine, and we went walking in the woods. On the way back we saw another monk and I recognized that he was someone visiting from another monastery. He came toward us, and there was something in his face that was beyond the shock of recognition. His eyes were open wide, and we looked at each other for the first time. I could imagine what the other monk was thinking: 'There goes Father Leo the hermit, all alone with a pretty girl. Well, perhaps that is a new slant on the hermit life.'

I angered a lot of people. I think the one I angered the most was the psychoanalyst I was seeing in Louisville, Jim Wygal. I would use his office for reading and writing when he was out of town or busy. One time she and I met at his office to talk and share a bottle of champagne. When he found out, he didn't bawl me out, but instead he ran her down. She had to suffer because I was a fool.

I would call her from the family guest house, knowing the calls went through the switchboard. We were bound to be overheard, sooner or later. Maybe I wanted to get caught, because I was torn between my love for her and my need for solitude. Getting caught solved the dilemma. We had talked of living together, my leaving the monastery, marrying, etc. It was preposterous. But I led her on, cruelly. Her beauty overwhelmed me. I don't know how else to describe it.

I longed for it madly. I could be with her for hours and hours and not be tired of her for an instant. I never stopped loving her. The truth is, I got scared. There was no future in it. My future had to be as a monk and a solitary. It's impossible for me even to dream about loving another woman. Impossible!

September 26 / Meat Cove

The ten-mile stretch of rough, unpaved road turned muddy with the early morning thaw. At the end of it was a small, blue tent by the edge of a high cliff.

Farther up the hill, near the woods, a trailer house, yellow, with brown trim, was pitched against the incline.

A man was busy taking apart an engine, pieces scattered on a table. He did not look up as you approached.

The table was level, with two legs dug deep into the ground. The man said something you could not understand and held up his dirty hands for you to see.

You wanted to shake his hand but he wouldn't let you. He had the good looks, the bright, easy smile, the strong body of a movie actor, which translated, in a place so cut off and remote, into a natural authority over people, animals, trees, the fishes of the sea, maybe the sea itself.

When he saw her coming up the hill, he became very conscious of his hands and began to rub them furiously up and down the front of his overalls.

She laughed and said never mind, but he held up his black, grease-covered hands and wouldn't let her come any closer.

She said something about the fantastic view, but he wasn't listening or didn't want to hear it.

What can I do for you folks, he said.

We'd like to do a bit of hiking in those woods, she said.

He looked at her, trying to figure her out. She was dressed for hiking, in jeans and walking shoes, with a nice leather jacket that failed to cover her narrow hips and tight ass.

She liked to show off her tight ass, aware of your every glance.

Let me guess. You want to see what it's like back in there, and maybe after that you'll come back and you'll build a cabin and you'll stay awhile.

She did not deny it. He did not try to conceal the disdain he felt for outsiders who show up at his door without knowledge or resources.

You wanted to hike overland to Lowland Cove. On the map you had been looking at – the one she kept in the glove compartment of the car – it appeared to be directly across from Meat Cove.

To return you would want to stay near the water, hugging the coastline.

He looked at you a moment without saying anything, not exactly in awe. He asked your name, his tone of voice suggesting that he would not answer any more questions until he knew it.

David Moosehunter, you replied without batting an eyelash. This is my guide and traveling companion, Elizabeth St. Clair.

His name was Peter, he said. He was a fisherman, a logger, a handyman, a bus driver, an experienced woodsman.

He was concerned for the woman's safety. She should not to go into the woods unless she was an experienced hiker, or unless she had a reliable guide. He looked at you and shook his head.

Clearly, you did not fill the bill.

It's not the woods that are dangerous, he said. It's the ones who go hiking in the woods who don't know what they're doing. They are fools. It doesn't matter how smart they think they are.

You laughed at this because he was right.

It is a vast area, he said, the last really wild corner of Nova Scotia. Nothing to be trifled with.

He was smiling as if tickled beyond imagining by something that you and she had yet to comprehend. There were black bears back in there, ready to knock you down and sit on you. There were cougars that would jump you from behind.

His eyes danced merrily.

Inside the house a phone rang. A young man with the high cheekbones, dark eyes, and dark hair of an Indian appeared behind the screen door.

In a flat voice he said something about a man named Louis who would like to talk. In the door the skin of his face had the flaked grey of a fine black and white photograph. In jeans and a white dress shirt he was tall and dark and very striking.

Peter continued his conversation with you, ignoring the young man. He knew a trail that would get you from where you were to Lowland Cove in three hours.

You were halfway down the hill to the car to get the map you had referred to earlier when you heard his voice, loud and angry, directed toward the young man in the door. Tell Louis he can go screw himself.

The young man disappeared inside the house again. Everything was quiet while you continued down the hill to the car.

From above, the car seemed to be parked right at the very edge of the cliff, ready to tumble over. In fact, though, it was a good fifteen feet away.

You rolled the map tight and held it aloft like a torch, as you climbed back up the steep, grassy hillside. Peter helped you spread the map on the table to get a better look. You stood on one side of him. She stood on the other.

With a word here, a word there, with animal grunts for emphasis, he showed you the way through the woods to your destination.

She plunged into the woods, and you had to hurry to catch up. When you were deep into the woods you began to see things you had never seen before – a timber wolf, a black panther, and a grey mare – ahead of you on the root-infested, soggy path.

She had such a strong step, strong and light at the same time, almost a spring, that you saw that she was as much animal as human. Sometimes, at home, she was a bird, a hawk, fighting for her share of whatever provision there was, for herself and her young. Her bony face, her hooked nose reinforced this image.

Walking ahead of you in the woods, though, bounding ahead of you in her low-cut, cushioned black walking shoes, her red socks, her faded blue jeans, she was a timber wolf. The haunted, pinhole eyes when they looked at you aroused an equal measure of affection and fear.

You remembered the young man in the screen door. Without the white dress shirt, bare-breasted, he was a black panther. You tried to imagine what his name was.

Eagle. His name was Eagle. He faded from sight, stepping back into the house.

You remembered the woman you had fallen in love with in Louisville two years ago. You remembered walking with her in the woods above the monastery.

She was a grey mare. Leading her through the woods to your favourite lake you were her stallion, her Andalusian, her King.

As you climbed higher above Meat Cove the trees were older and larger, balsam fir, red spruce, yellow birch, red maple. It was late September. It was 'carnival time' – when the leaves of the hardwoods, losing their green, reveal yellow and orange, purple and scarlet.

After a hard, hour-long climb, over dry, rocky slopes, and wet, soggy hollows, you came to a clearing at the top of a hill. The little settlement of Meat Cove now lay far below, so far that the two houses, just back from the cliff, one white, one yellow, were no bigger than dots on the green hillside.

At the edge of the woods, the sea, farther out, sparkled in the bright, mid-day sun. In the distance it was a sheet of silver.

The forest through which she was taking you, on your way downhill to Lowland Cove, was mostly evergreen, spruce and jack pine. It was a thick, dark, lonely forest, more remote than any you had ever traveled through, the perfect place, you thought, where priests could be sent when they are in disgrace as punishment.

This might be ideal for me. It is so lonely. But I'm beginning to wonder if this whole search for perfect solitude might not be a subtle form of self-punishment.

She was leading the way, keeping as close to the path as she could, though in places it was covered and obscured by a fresh fall of pine needles and leaves.

She could hear you thinking.

Without looking back she said, What if you get sick? What if you fall down and break a leg? No one would ever find you. Be practical.

But your idea of what is practical may not be the same as the next person's, you said. The practical thing for you in your mind was to get lost somewhere. The only way they could find you would be by boat. Days, weeks, months would go by, and no one would come. That would be cool.

It might also be suicide, she suggested.

As for suicide, you said, I would not mind dropping dead here on the spot.

You don't mean that, she said.

I do, but I'm afraid it's not in the cards. It's not allowed. More is the pity.

Where the path swung left and down a hill she turned and faced you. What is it you want?

Through and beyond the trees you could see flashes of water, and you knew that whatever else might await you Lowland Cove was close at hand.

Something much harder than anything I've ever experienced before, you said to her. Something hard enough and sharp enough to split open this cold heart of mine and get at the reality of who I am.

We all need to be alone at times, she said. It's what keeps us sane.

She began to talk about her need to be alone, about me, about how I hated it when she went away on retreat, to be by herself. She wanted to know what you thought. Was I fucked up?

You shrugged your shoulders. How were you supposed to know? You'd only just met me. People are complex.

She said she would tell you just how fucked up I was, if you would wanted to know.

Sure, you said, fire away.

She walked ahead a little, and stopped again, under the pine trees. You came around and stood in front of her, your back to the water. She was going to give you her version of things. It was not your business to correct her. Only to listen.

When we bought the house on the hill above the bay, she began, it was on the understanding that I would have one room I could call my own. I was thrilled because since childhood I had never had a room of my own. With two children, I was going a little crazy. Henry always had his room, where he could read and prepare lectures. I had nowhere to go, unless I locked myself up in the bathroom.

I don't think Henry really understood, but he agreed. I got the spare bedroom at the end of the hall, but that was okay. It was mine, which meant I could do anything I wanted. If I wanted to paint it pink, I could paint it pink. Best of all there was a window looking out on the water.

In the end I did not paint it pink. I painted it a very pale yellow, a lemon yellow. I painted the ceiling was off-white. Everything was bare, minimal. On one wall was a death mask I had made a long time ago, at a workshop somewhere in Vermont. On another wall was a print showing Vishnu and his consort, in a blissful and explicit union of body forms. A record of John Cage played over and over.

The room was a place of quiet and meditation. Everything was fine that first winter. In April I was called away for a week, to look after my mother who was ill. When I got back, everything was changed. A colleague had returned to campus after a year teaching in Japan. Without checking with me, without even mentioning it on the phone when we talked, Henry had let the man have my room.

Just for a couple of weeks, a month at the most, Henry explained, until the man could find a new apartment. I was so mad I couldn't talk. It felt like I had been raped. Without my permission, he had entered a space that had been mine alone.

After that I never felt alone in that room. It was no longer mine. It had been defiled. So I gave it up. I took down the death mask. I took down the print of Vishnu. I took down the little altar I had set up, with a candle and incense.

It was the worst kind of violation, because it showed he did not respect my right to draw my own boundaries. What it told me was that he would do whatever he wanted if it suited him. He would take it upon himself to decide right and wrong.

What did he say, when he saw that you were so badly hurt?

He said he couldn't see what all the fuss was about. After all, he'd changed the sheets.

What a thing to say.

And he hadn't touched anything, which wasn't even true, because someone had burned a stick of incense and left the match on the sill.

There aren't too many things I'd fight for, but privacy is one of them.

You wanted to tell her that she was being too harsh. But that was the last thing she wanted to hear, you knew.

At the edge of the hard Cape Breton earth it was scrub bush and rock and loneliness. The highland jutted out into the ocean itself. A stream without a name cascaded down and flowed between banks of round, grey, polished stones to the ocean.

This was Lowland Cove. You thought you might build here, high on the hill. You would have everything – forest, sky, ocean, the setting sun.

It was a beautiful spot, she agreed.

The air was cold now, in the late-afternoon sun. The wind was gusting out of the west, across the gulf. As the sun fell the sea looked more green than blue. Even the green was more grey than green.

The wind, whistling low, broke the tops of the waves, so that, as far as the eye could see, the water was dense with flecks of jagged white.

As you made your way back through the scrub bush, over the smooth rock on the high cliff at Cape St. Lawrence in the gathering dark you were silent.

October 2 / Danger

She felt out of sorts from the moment she opened the door. She was alone, shunned. No one came in, no one even looked in the window.

She tried reading, but she could not keep her mind on the words. They ran on and on without making any sense.

At eleven thirty a familiar face entered the store, a second-year college student who had begun to frequent the store, with one odd request after another. Hitler was his obsession. On principle she did not stock books about Hitler, but Sean would not take no for an answer.

Guten Tag Mein Frau, he said, pulling the door closed behind him with a bang. I know how much that annoys you but I need the practice.

I do not have *Mein Kampf*, she said, delivering a pre-emptive strike.

Ach du lieber.

I do not have any books by Hitler. I do not have any books about Hitler.

You say that, and I'm sure you believe it but I'm here to prove you wrong.

I know my stock.

Tell me this then, do you have a book called *Also Sprach Zarathustra?*

Nietzsche has nothing to do with Hitler. Nietzsche is a philosopher, a metaphysician.

Yeah and Hitler was a metamaniac, I know, but they both believed in what we have come to know as *Der Übermensch.*

I doubt if Hitler believed in anything except his own genius.

He believed in the greatness of Germany.

If he believed in the greatness of Germany, then why did he do everything in his power to destroy Germany.

No need to get angry. I'm just a lowly student, asking dumb questions.

I'm not angry.

Then why are you shouting at me.

I'm not shouting at you.

I think I'll buy the Nietzsche and get out of here before I get killed.

The Nietzsche is not for sale.

I saw a copy when I was in yesterday.

That was my personal copy.

I get the message. You wish I'd stop bugging you.

Yes.

One day I will, don't worry.

Good.

One last question. What is that music you're listening to?

It's called 'Harold in Italy.'

I like it. It's nice.

I don't think *nice* is the word.

I'm going, I'm going. Auf wiedersehn.

Good-bye.

Did I ever tell you, I think you're a nice woman.

Good-bye.

Let's talk about something else next time besides Hitler.

I'm hoping there won't be a next time.

Touché.

Frazzled, she looked for the pocketbook she had been reading. It was a copy of your *Conjectures of a Guilty Bystander*.

Inside the front cover, on the title page, someone had scribbled in pencil, 'Good Book.' At the top was a stamp, in red ink, saying 'Georgina Thomson Branch.'

She opened the book at random and read.

Winter. Shakertown. Marvelous, vast, silent, white open spaces around the old buildings, put up by the Shakers at Pleasant Hill a hundred or a hundred and fifty years ago. Already a hundred years ago, about the time of the Civil War, the Shakers reached their peak and began to decline. Cold, pure light. Some great old trees. I took some photographs but it was so cold my finger could no longer feel the shutter release. Marvelous subjects. I have no way of explaining how the bare, blank side of an old frame house with some broken windows can be so indescribably beautiful. The Shaker builders, like all their craftsmen, had the gift of achieving perfect forms. There is nothing so good anywhere in Kentucky. Those few moments of eloquent silence in the snow stay with me, follow me home, do not go away.

She closed the book, then opened it again, at random.

Solitude has its own special work, a deepening awareness that the world needs, a struggle against alienation. True solitude is deeply aware of the world's needs. It does not hold the world at arm's length.

By mid-afternoon, having taken in a little over thirty dollars, she was already in a bad mood when I called.

I have a question for you, I said, in a voice that reminded her of the recently departed Sean.

Is Thanksgiving next Monday or the Monday after next?

Look at your calendar.

I don't have a calendar.

Why not?

No one gave me one this year.

Then go out and buy one.

Can we just stick to the question.

Thanksgiving is the Monday after next. Why?

I want to invite someone.

Who?

A colleague. You haven't met him. He's new.

Is he nice?

He's very nice. He plays the guitar and sings.
Maybe he'll sing for you.

How very sexy.

Unfortunately he already has a wife.

I suppose she's a poet or something.

She paints.

Houses?

No, canvases.

How very artsy-fartsy.

What do you say?

Fine with me. Invite Chuck and Barbara too.
Invite Jack and Margie. I'll be in Ottawa that weekend.

Ottawa?

We had this discussion about a month ago.

No we didn't.

Try to remember. If I say *Ottawa Book Fair,*

does that ring a bell?

Shit.

Go buy a calendar. You might remember these things.

What am I supposed to do now? I've already more or less told him we'd spend Thanksgiving together.

Start shopping, dear Henry, start shopping.

It's not the shopping I'm worried about, it's the cooking.

Never too late to learn.

Do me a favour. Write down your favourite recipe and let's sit down tonight and talk about it. Tell me what I need to know.

Glad to.

Good God, I mean cooking is just not my thing. I know more about the planet Jupiter than I do about cooking.

Thanksgiving is just about the easiest meal you could think of.

No, I can think of something a lot easier. Try breakfast.

I can do the yams and the cranberry sauce and the pecan pie before I leave, so relax.

It's not the yams I'm worried about, it's the goddamn turkey.

A bird is just a bird.

What's that supposed to mean?

A turkey's like a chicken, only bigger.

Thanks.

I hung up. She hung up.

Left alone she wandered to the back of the store. She felt dizzy.

In the mirror on the wall next to the bookcase jammed with illustrated children's books she saw the face of a 48-year-old woman with shockingly hollow cheeks and large dark eyes that would not stop roaming.

She heard voices in her head – your voice, your laughter.

When you laughed, she swooned. She no longer knew where she was or who she was.

She closed early. There were three steps down to the sidewalk. On the second step she felt a strong surge of vertigo. She *wanted* to fall.

She told herself that she would never again set foot in the store. She could not continue living as before. She must look for you until she found you.

She thought about the children. What would happen to them? Who would take care of them?

In the car on the way home she found the answer she had been looking for. After the book fair I will just keep going. They will think I lost my memory and wandered off. They will miss me for a while, and then they will forget.

On the sidewalk in front of the house, rummaging in her bag for her key, she whispered to herself. It will be as if I fell down and hit my head and forgot who I was.

In the hallway outside the room where the children were watching television, she stopped. He does not know the danger he's in.

I must go now. I must warn him. There's so little time.

October 24 / Not Limited to Form

The dull dusk was beginning to show the dark that rimmed the hills beyond Chittagong. When a voice announced the approach to the airport she sat forward, leaning into the small, curved, milky-green window.

She felt the plane dip down and the clouds rip by, obscuring her vision. Trapped in the clouds, she felt small, lost. Touching her forehead lightly to the window, she saw that the clouds were moving – fast, fast. Not the plane, not she.

The plane did not exist. She herself did not exist. Only this rapid movement of cloud in a space without end.

The movement of cloud in space sucked everything away with it. Everything dissolved into dust, into water.

Alarm bells went off somewhere in her brain. She did not like herself for fearing what fate held in store for her. Don't forget the really real, she told herself.

A stewardess came by, checking seat belts.

When she sat back she felt a pain as sharp as a knife at the bottom of the rib cage where she had once torn a muscle lifting a box of books. She was stiff and tight, from three days of travel and waiting at airports – in Ottawa, Chicago, San Francisco, Honolulu, Tokyo, Bangkok.

She had arrived in Bangkok on Wednesday, October 23, but had had to stay overnight because the flight to Calcutta had been cancelled. On Thursday, the 24th, she had spent the morning at the Temple of the Emerald Buddha, sightseeing.

She was too overwhelmed to do anything but sightsee.

The flight to Calcutta had finally departed that evening, two hours late.

Below the clouds Calcutta looked clean and alive, with white lights everywhere lighting up the dark. The plane flew north along the river Hooghly, then turned back toward a landing at the airport.

It was only at a certain height, a few hundred feet above the ground, that her fear of falling came into play. She no longer dared to look. Nakhoda Mosque, its central dome burning bright in the night, passed below, unseen.

With ice cold hands she reached into her bag for a book to read. If she could concentrate on the book she would not be afraid of falling.

It was a paperback copy of *The Way of Chuang*

Tzu. She read softly to herself.

All that is limited by form, semblance, sound, colour, is called 'object.' Among them all, man alone is more than an object. And though, like objects, he has form and semblance, he is not limited to form. He is more. He can attain to formlessness.

As the plane descended, her reading became a sort of chanting. He is not limited to form, she repeated to herself.

The Indian woman in the seat next to her looked at her for the first time since boarding in Bangkok. Be careful what you wish, she said. Who knows, you may come back as some sort of insect.

Caught between her fear of heights and her sense of being under attack from an unexpected quarter, she was angrier than she knew. I don't believe I was speaking to you.

The plane touched down, with two or three bounces beyond what might have been expected. The Indian woman had a way of sniffing to show that it did not matter to her in the least, if they crashed or if they failed to crash. Her eyes were an intense brown, as clear as a child's. She was young, perhaps twenty-five, but with the haughty self-assurance of one much older.

The ride to the terminal was as bumpy as a dirt road. She waited for the building to come into sight. Do you live here, she asked.

Not in a million years, the Indian woman said. I live in Bangkok. I'm here to meet a friend and do some shopping. What brings you?

Funny, I'm here to meet a friend too.

I suppose that your friend, like mine, is attending the so-called Temple of Understanding Conference.

She began frantically flicking the front of her white cotton turtleneck, as if brushing away flies. Her hard nipples hurt. This really is extraordinary, she said.

The plane stopped fifty feet short of the building. Two men in shirt-sleeves, each one thinner than a rope, pushed a set of steps toward the front door of the plane.

A happy coincidence I would say, the Indian woman grinned.

You can call it a coincidence if you want. Personally I don't believe in coincidences.

Ah, I see. A sort of total embrace whereby you become more Indian than the actual Indian. Very well, let's say there are no coincidences. It was written in the stars that our paths should cross. Come with me then, let me show you this city I love to hate.

Right now?

Don't be insane. Do you know what time it is?

Do you know how tired I am? In the morning. Please.

They moved toward the front of the plane, Lise close behind the other woman, surprised to find that she was an inch taller, though she herself was only five feet five.

Her toes felt naked in the new sandals she had picked up at the airport in San Francisco during a stop-over. Where shall we meet?

Where are you staying?

At a hotel near the Indian Museum, on Park Street.

Meet me on the steps of the museum at ten o'clock. My friend has another day of meetings. So does yours, I presume. I have some shopping I want to do. Otherwise I'm yours. Do with me what you will.

Shall I bring my camera?

That would be asking for trouble.

Not once, but a hundred times she had planned this entry into Calcutta.

She had thought about it many times, going over all the details of it. She had made it the focus of her meditation sessions at home in Nova Scotia.

She had collected books and newspaper clippings about Calcutta and places to stay in Calcutta and in other cities on the Ganges as far away as Banares. In the room where she meditated she had hung a poster of the Jain Temple in Calcutta, showing the front steps, the huge columns of pink stone, the glittering mirrors leading far into the mysterious, hazy interior.

When she climbed the steps of the museum and turned to look along Chowringhee in the direction of Nakhoda Mosque, she saw that everything was as it should be. The flood of humanity, the rickshaws in an endless stream, the cows lying undisturbed on the sidewalk, the children in rags, begging – it was all as she had foreseen.

There was only one element that her mental picture was lacking – the Indian woman she had met on the airplane from Bangkok. But when she looked up the steps toward the museum she saw her standing there, waving and smiling, as if she had appeared out of thin air.

The blue sky tilted to reveal billowy clouds that were whiter than any white she had ever seen. Gone completely was the haughty, contemptuous look. In a long, flowing, pale-yellow sari, with the material pushed up above the elbows, she looked relaxed and at the same time very much in control. Her black hair was brushed back and tied loosely at the neck. The wing of her nose was pierced with a gold ring that glittered in the bright sun.

Her name was Aloka, but she preferred to be called Loki. In blue jeans and a white polo shirt Lise was ready, she believed, for the heat of the day and the press of the crowd.

Loki suggested a walk through the park, the Maidan, opposite the museum, then a stop for lunch at the Eden Gardens. On the other side of the park, a little girl followed them along Chowringhee and into the park, murmuring something like, Mommy, Mommy, I am very poor, until Lise finally stopped and looked at her.

She had big innocent eyes and a perfect smile. She stretched out her hand. The smile remained fixed, adamant. Lise could not say no.

Okay, it's a contest, she knew, but the fact is she

was very poor.

As soon as this one had moved away, a dozen more appeared.

Scat, Loki hissed, and they did.

I haven't the heart, Lise said.

Remember one thing. They will take the shirt from your back if you let them. It's best not to listen. What you do not hear cannot hurt you.

A hard teaching.

A necessary teaching.

Ahead was the main road through the park. To the south they had a sweeping view of the Victoria Memorial. They turned north, toward the Ochterlony Monument, half a mile away, just visible above a stand of tall, stately palm trees.

Lise, who had the legs and the stride of a long-distance runner, wanted to get moving, but Loki kept to the same slow pace.

Lise said the first thing that came into her mind. Tell me about that job of yours in Bangkok.

It's a job. What can I say?

Let me guess. You work on population control.

In a round-about way, I suppose I do. We work on economic development. We give technical advice on projects designed first and foremost to augment local self-sufficiency. Economic development slows the rate of the population growth. I believe that's true in every case that's been studied – India, China, even Africa.

India seems to be growing very fast, wouldn't you say?

India is a very hard nut to crack, I will have to admit. In China you've got a central government with authority and the might to back it up.

Too much authority, many would say.

Maybe. But listen, tell me about this mysterious friend you've come to meet.

His name is Thomas Merton. He's a Roman Catholic monk. He's also a poet and a student of Eastern religions.

A man of many talents, it would seem.

He's also a fierce critic of America, and its never-ending war. I think they'd like to kill him for that.

I suppose you're in love with this monk.

Love is not the word I'd use. We've shared several past lives together.

I thought Catholics do not believe in reincarnation.

They don't. That's one of the reasons I'm not a Catholic. One among many.

What about your Thomas Merton?

He's a Catholic. What can I say? He doesn't believe me.

Ah, I see, he belongs to you, whether he knows it or not.

Only if he chooses it. In my philosophy everything is a matter of free choice. Nothing is pre-determined. We come in with karmic potential but nothing is fixed.

The table that Loki had reserved at the Eden Gardens was outside, in an area of fine, white gravel in the shade of several tall, hundred-year-old teak trees, scattered in a sort of half-circle. The view was west, toward the Hooghly.

The waitress, who looked forty, wore a strawberry red sari over a white, close-fitting blouse. The meal began simply enough, with thinly sliced carrots, in a seasoning of safflower oil and bitter herbs.

Loki wanted to know how Lise had come to believe in reincarnation.

I can't say how or when or where, it's just something I've lived.

Maybe it's all in your imagination

What is imagination? The mind pictures something to itself, but if the mind is all there is, then what the mind pictures to itself must also be real.

I see, the doctrine of mind-only. But tell me this. If I imagine a lion coming toward me, between two of these nice tall trees, does that mean I should be afraid, that I should get up and run?

We can be afraid and not have to run from our fear. A lion that we see in our imagination is a different kind of lion. It may represent the forces that are threatening the life of the soul. That's very real, don't you think?

Maybe this lion stops and gives you a friendly smile. Then what?

That would mean that the soul is in a healthy state and does not need to be afraid.

You have the answer to everything. For myself I believe it is wiser not to know the answer always.

Loki's sharp words stung Lise. She looked around, for a way out if required.

The waitress came toward them across the court with a smile that seemed friendly enough until you looked more closely and saw the fixed, dull aspect. The dahl, in thick, cherry red bowls with rolled lips, was grey, lumpy, nearly tasteless.

I believe it is wiser to ask the right question than to have the right answer. When you always have the right answer, it cuts off a good discussion.

Lise felt sick. I'm so very sorry, she said, but like everything else she said this came out sounding false.

No need to be sorry. Loki scooped the dahl into

her mouth cradled in a piece of thin bread.

How did you come to work for the UN, Lise asked in her fury.

That is a very long story.

I'm not asking you to begin at the beginning.

As a rule I don't talk about my life. It's not a very interesting life, I've discovered.

I don't believe you.

I've learned many things working for the UN but I think the most important is that I'm not the centre of the universe.

Strange that you of all people would say that. Everything I've learned in the last while makes me think that each of us *is* the centre of the universe.

How do you mean?

The part of us that's really real contains the whole universe. You need to learn to think beyond your normal, everyday self.

Ah, I see, the idea of the Atmen, the Higher Self. I congratulate you for having done your homework.

I feel sad for you because you've lost part of your heritage.

You have no understanding of the Hindu. The Hindu is always adding to his heritage, never subtracting.

From the white-framed, screen door at the back

of the kitchen the waitress came forward once more, with the main course. She seemed to float toward them, like one who had no care and no concern in the world save for the moment.

The plate of chicken curry with parsleyed potatoes and chutney was for Lise, the plate of fish curry with steamed rice and chutney for Loki.

I'd like pepper, Lise said. Freshly ground.

The waitress bowed and backed away.

She wanted to be alone. She wanted to see Calcutta alone, with fresh eyes, not mediated. She wondered why she had agreed to meet Loki in the first place. Loki seemed to have no other aim in mind except to insult her.

I find you a difficult person.

There's something so very false about you, You're the kind of person who talks a lot about soul and love and light but always it's a grabbing and clutching for glory.

I have to go now. Lise rose from the table.

Don't play the fool. It is very unwise to go out in this crazy city on your own. Add to that the fact that you're a woman and the additional fact that you're wearing clothes that blare out, I'm from the West and I'm so very fucking rich, and you might not get back to the hotel in one piece.

I'll take my chances.

Go then, fine with me. Good riddance too.

The dessert arrived, in a glass bowl was a small helping of a plain, white unsweetened yoghurt, set very firm, with no run off. Sweating big drops of sweat, her mouth burning from the hot curry, Lise came close to swallowing her pride and returning to the table.

But it was the little laugh that Loki and the waitress shared that finally chased her away.

October 25 / Howrah Bridge

The blaring of the ships on the Hooghly seemed closer and closer as she hurried along the street toward Howrah Bridge. The sounds from dockside were like an assault to her senses as she approached the bridge.

The traffic on the street became so congested, so noisy that she thought there must have been an accident. She was engulfed in a tide of people coming toward her and turning in all directions.

A small monk-like figure stood as if he had been waiting for her all day. For one American penny, he said, he would lay hands on her and for another he would pour a drop of holy Ganges water into her mouth.

There was such a burning in her throat that she cried with relief as she dug into the pockets of her jeans for the coins. The crowd pushed the monk past her, on down the street.

Was she dreaming? Everywhere there were rickshaws, transporting people or merchandise. Coolies hurried along with baskets and packages piled up on their heads, their faces showing the strain. She was trapped by the crowd and pushed onto the bridge and in the direction of Howrah.

Along the side of the bridge an unbroken line of vendors squatted on the ground behind their goods. There were six lanes of traffic. Vehicles of every description were stuck in a gigantic traffic-jam.

Trucks gunned their engines in an attempt to move forward. Red double-decker buses, overloaded with people, leaned over at such extreme angles that they looked as if at any moment they would tip over altogether. Herds of cows, goats, and buffalo, driven along with sticks, made their way in and out of the labyrinth of vehicles.

Poor beasts, she cried to herself, pressing her hands to her eyes so as not to see. The sensation was so welcome that she pressed still harder.

With the tips of her fingers she could feel the hard bones of her forehead.

Funny, this is where I live, she thought to herself. In here.

She stopped fighting the throbbing behind her eyes. Something in her view of the universe shifted. She no longer felt any pain or even discomfort.

Stars of every colour danced in a black field.

She remembered standing on the road in front of her house with her father when she was six, looking up at a sky full of stars.

All the colours came together and formed one

huge red ball in the middle of her forehead. She lived in this energy field, not in this body.

There was a sensation of intense heat. Then it was as if she were falling from a great height – from an airplane, or from the clouds, into the sea below.

The loud cry she heard, from a woman selling combs and into whose cart she fell, seemed to come to her from underwater, like the cry of a whale who has lost her mate.

October 28 / Older Than the Mountains

The day you departed for New Delhi, Monday, October 28, she was well enough to leave her hotel for the first time since fainting on the Howrah Bridge at noon on Friday. All weekend she had felt alone and afraid.

She could not face the idea of going out again into that mass of hot, sweaty bodies.

She slept more than she had slept in weeks. She drifted in and out of consciousness.

She let her hand rest on the table by the side of the bed, on top of the stack of books she had brought with her from San Francisco – *Tropic of Cancer*, *Delta of Venus*, *Naked Lunch*, and *Nightwood*.

Her hand flat, palm up. The books collected dust.

Sunday evening, sitting on the floor before a candle, she tried to meditate. Her mind was troubled. She could find no centre, no focus, no still point. She had difficulty breathing.

Something was dragging at her from a part of herself that she did not know and did not want to know. Something dark, something half-formed was reaching out for her, to drag her down.

She had fled husband, children, friends, country, only to find – this emptiness.

You were always one step ahead of her. A call to the Birla Academy where you had been asked to give a talk alerted her to the fact that you were going to be out of town for two weeks.

In answer to her question the sing-song voice at the other end of the line told her that you would return after two weeks to catch a plane north to Darjeeling.

No, you would not be staying overnight but would go north without delay.

As in a dream she jumped ahead in her mind to what she must do. She would fly to Darjeeling before you and wait for you there. When she saw you, she would ask you to take her with you into the mountains.

If you loved her, you would take her with you into the mountains. You would find a place for her where she could live in solitude and perfect harmony, the same as you. On the side of a mountain, very high up, you would help her find a simple hut where she could live, like the monks of Tibet.

She would live alone in the hut, until you came again.

At a newsstand on Chowringhee, next to the Indian Museum, she bought a map of Darjeeling. A sign on the wall said, Are you hot, refresh yourself with raisins.

She wanted something cold and wet, not sweet. The cashier said that there was a vendor on the sidewalk below the museum, selling cokes.

In the brisk winds of the approaching cyclone and under the darkening sky, the vendor was nowhere to be seen.

She crossed Chowringhee and fought her way along the Maidan, against the wind. The rain fell steadily. There were fewer people on the street than might have been expected even in bad weather.

Her hair became thoroughly wet. Her clothes clung to her body. The skin of her forehead seemed to melt away to reveal raw, protruding bone.

She felt that she was more bone than flesh. At the entrance to the park she stopped. She let the rain come down. She was completely drenched.

After a few minutes she turned and went back to the hotel.

She slept again until dark, and woke in a daze, unsure if it was early or late.

She sat in a chair by the window, in the dark, listened to the hooting of the boats on the river beyond the block of warehouses.

She picked up one of the books she had brought

along – the novel *Nightwood*. She read without much interest and felt very dull until suddenly a line jumped out at her. In the same way as the character Jenny accused Robin of 'sensuous communication with unclean spirits' she accused herself of forcing her attentions on you at a time when you were unconscious of your own sensuality.

The more she followed you and would not let you go, the more she felt she was hounding you to your death. But she could not help herself.

It was not you that she was down and rubbing noses with but some dirty dog off the streets of Calcutta, some dark and unclean shadow of the one you really embodied.

She had to get out of this city of sorrow and joy if she did not want to die. Darjeeling held the key for her. But the door that was about to open and the mystery that she was about to vanish inside of she did not want to think about, just yet.

From the plane the high mountains were visible above the clouds. Kanchenjunga was the closest. Several hundred miles away was Everest, with a dark side, a shadow as immense as some countries.

Directly below, it could be California as easily as India. But she went over the Ganges, and the descent left her cold and dejected.

From the airport it was a four-hour ride up the mountain to Darjeeling. On a very bad road with the potential for many landslides.

The city itself was a fraudulent copy of something that once was fabulous – English hats, tweeds, walking sticks, St. Joseph's College, and so on. The Windermere was really called Windamere she found out.

She was so exhausted that she fell across her bed without undressing. When she woke, sometime before dawn, she had a very bad sore throat. She looked in her handbag for an aspirin.

She was so miserable she no longer thought about seeing you. If she saw you now she would be too weak to think of anything to say. The conviction that she was not good enough for you gripped her heart as tightly as the cold gripped her throat.

She was not able to think of a thing that she was good for, except one thing.

At the office she learned that you planned to stay at the Windamere. She asked which room but was told this was private.

Maybe you would stay in the room next to hers or in the room across the hall. The idea frightened her. Everything frightened her.

If she saw you now you would be like a

stranger. She longed for the high and wind-swept mountains.

The rains had caused many landslides around Darjeeling. She hired a cab and said that she wanted to go out and see the devastation.

Very bad floods, the driver said. Many hills washed away. Plenty of devastation.

If she picked the Mim Tea Plantation, it was because the road climbed a sculpted hillside that reminded her of the care she had taken in sculpting her own destiny, and the control she had exercised in everything large and small.

How tired she was now.

At the entrance to the plantation she dismissed the driver. She stood waving as he started back down the hill.

She set off on foot, on the winding road above and behind the main house, away from the noise and the dirt and the contamination of all that is human. She climbed to the top of the hill.

Above the last of the giant hemlock, above the last of the cultivated fields, across the deep valley the mountain was horribly gashed, where whole sections of forest had been washed away.

She found her mind rebelling against the landslides.

She thought of reforestation projects and other ways to deny them, forbid them.

She wanted this all to be permanent.

The sun was high overhead, inexplicably cool. Far down, as if inside the hollow earth, was the clear, sweet sound of a temple bell.

Voices of children on the mountainside below her, near the main house, brought tears to her eyes. Everything fell into place.

The mountains will fall, the rivers will dry up, but there will always be the sound of a temple bell. There will always be the voices of children.

Nothing bad can happen because nothing is what it appears to be. What appears to be bad one moment turns into something good the next moment.

Everything is what you make of it. There is nothing to worry about.

She dozed in the warm sun, in the wild, fragrant field.

In a dream she saw the face of her driver that morning, a toothless old man with a wrinkled face like dried leather. She saw the way he pursed his lips when he spoke. She saw the glint in his eye.

She leaned into the window of the cab to hear what he was saying. I'm older than the mountains, he whispered. Better looking too, he added with a toothless laugh.

The voices of the children in the field below woke her. Getting to her feet, she remembered nothing but her resolution.

She walked across the field behind the Mim Tea Plantation. She was weightless, as if she had already left the body.

Across the valley, beyond the deeply scarred mountains that were close as close can be, she saw Kanchenjunga for the first time above the clouds. She saw the pure beauty of its shape and outline, all in white.

She heard a voice saying, There is another side of the mountain. She realized that it was turned around and she was seeing it from the Tibetan side.

The voices seemed to be getting closer, climbing toward her on the road that turned and twisted to the top of the hill.

At the edge of the cliff she could hear the wind in the trees below, softly whistling. It was like the wind she had heard so many times in the trees below the house where she lived in Nova Scotia, by the edge of the great sea.

She could hear the children laughing and calling to one another. When the moment was right, when the children were laughing loudest, she jumped.

Her mind was mercifully empty. She felt no

fear.

As she fell she remembered the life she had just lived as a past life. Someone else's life.

If she felt anything, it was a sense of wonder at what lay ahead.

Something struck her back. It seemed that her body was being thrown into the air, into distant space, very far and very fast, while all around her the sky was giving birth to star upon star.

Then one of these stars exploded. There was an immense flash of white. She was on fire, lifted up in the white-hot flux that flowed into the heart of the universe.

End of October / Slow Down

For the second time in two weeks Bengal was threatened with floods as a cyclone moved up from the south of India. Tall coconut palms moved against a grey sky.

Men and women stood on the balconies of apartment houses watching for the rains. Cows wandered the streets, as lost as the countless homeless.

You no longer knew where you were, only that your hosts, the Birlas, were driving you to see the schools, the hospital, and the elegant theatre that they had built.

The wind seemed to blow right through you, right through the car, right through the Birlas. The truth was that you did not care a nickel about the elegant theatre, or the hospital, or the schools.

The thing that was on your mind mostly was – girls. The evening of the twenty-fourth, a Thursday, you had a long and very good conversation with a young Jain laywoman from Bombay. Her name was Vatsala Amin.

You talked about the kind of meditation she was doing and about her master, Munishri Chitrabhanu. Her desire, she said, was to live in solitude in the Himalayas.

She was an extremely beautiful and spiritual person. You sat on the floor, listening to sitar music, and you fell in love with her great, soft, intelligent, dark eyes.

She was serious and lively, warm and spiritual, in her white sari. She looked like an angel.

For some unexplained reason she could not stay to the end of the conference, but had to leave immediately. The moment she was gone you missed her.

On Saturday, at the closing session, there were two girls in miniskirts, calling themselves Schotzy and Pattie, very sweet, and almost naked, naive and self-absorbed. They kept calling everything beautiful, beautiful – except when it was too square.

They wanted adventure – to go hiking in some woods, to get lost and wander into some village and stay up till dawn and smoke pot. It did not matter what happened, if they killed themselves or not, it was all so beautiful, so beautiful.

Slow down, you wanted to tell them, slow down. It won't be so beautiful when you're dead.

You wanted to hold them very tight and tell them they were very beautiful and very hip and very foolish.

Sunday morning you went with an American colleague, Sister Barbara Mitchell from Manhattanville College, to a private home to say Mass. It was simple and subdued and a welcome change of pace.

The cyclone was quite close now. Everyone was being warned for the third or fourth time. As you drove back to the hotel, you heard air-raid sirens being tested.

Everyone should get inside before it was too late. A disaster of one sort or another was imminent. It could be the approaching cyclone, or it could be the next war with Pakistan, whichever came first.

At the hotel you packed for your flight Monday to New Delhi. You were looking forward to your interview with the Dalai Lama, scheduled for November 4. You did not much care when the cyclone hit, before you left or after. It was all the same to you.

All you knew and all you needed to know was that the Dalai Lama was waiting.

You had a sense of the inevitability of everything that was happening, to yourself as well as everyone else.

December 14 / The Cause of Death

In the high, bare windows at the front of the recital room on the top floor of the old convent the first real snow of the season was beginning to fall. The flakes were large, fluffy, white specks, like swamp grass. They hardly fell at all, but floated or drifted upward, as if caught in an updraft of wind.

The wooden folding chairs in front of me, all in neat rows, all as hard as mine and just as narrow, were filling one by one, with hushed, anxious, uncommonly reserved parents. With trembling hands and queasy stomach I read Jason's name on the yellow, typed program.

Listed as number fourteen, he was scheduled to play two pieces, the Viennese Sonatina No. 1 in C major by Mozart and the Promenade Op. 65, No. 2 by Prokofieff. In a previous recital he had forgot his piece in mid-performance, and no one seemed to know what to do.

He came to a full stop, and for an agonizing ten seconds no one in the room had dared move or breathe, so complete was the apprehension of doom.

When he still could not go on, his teacher came forward with his musical score, with her own notes and with a nod of encouragement that was just as subtle as it was effective.

Without looking around or batting an eye he had begun again, where he had left off. But for the next two weeks he was in such a dark, foul mood that no one could speak to him.

I told myself how glad I was that Emma had decided to take violin. If you miss a note on the violin, you just keep sawing away. Everyone sounds terrible on the violin in the beginning. On the piano you are supposed to get a few notes right.

A short three months later he accepted the challenge of a second recital without a word of protest.

Several students drifted in now, Jason among them, looking for a place to sit where they might be invisible. They spoke to no one and moved slowly, as if drugged.

As if none of this had anything to do with them in the least.

I wish they'd get on with it before I feel really sick, I thought, not realizing I was also saying the words out loud.

The woman in the seat in front of me, a thirty-something woman with thin shoulders, in a white cotton turtleneck that fit too tightly for comfort, her long brown hair combed straight, reaching the small of her back, looked around at me, surprise and disapproval in her eyes.

Something hot spread up the back of my neck, into the bones behind my ears and into my temples. I looked away, toward the door where people were still coming in and out. I recognized no one.

I let my mind drift back to the newspaper clipping that I had come across that morning. Under the heading 'International News', almost buried at the bottom of one of the pages in the back I had found the following short notice:

The Trappist monk, Thomas Merton, has died in Bangkok, Thailand. The cause of death was apparently a heart attack occasioned by the touching of a defective electrical fan. Affectionately known as Father Louie, Thomas Merton was the author of numerous books, including his best-selling autobiography. In Bangkok to attend a conference on monastic renewal, he died on Tuesday, December 10, within hours of giving an invited talk.

Perched on the edge of the piano bench, a young girl began to play her piece, just barely recognizable as 'This Old Man.' In the program her name was given as Colleen Brophy. No trophy for this little angel. Sorry.

Letting the news of your death sink in, I felt strangely euphoric. With your death there was a chance that Lise would come home.

She had left everything, husband, children, etc., to follow you to Asia. I did not blame you. What blame can be found in a man for merely existing, merely being himself? Yet of course I did blame you, because you were the precipitating agent.

By the time I looked up again, the recital was well under way. A boy about ten was playing the cello. In the program his name was listed as Robin Armstrong.

His piece was called 'Sweet Melody' authored by one S. Fletcher. It was, sadly, anything but sweet, and his arm, poor player, was anything but strong.

If I kept my eyes closed, I could just hear the music hidden in the noise. I could see the blue sky above the dark clouds.

In the window it was still snowing. It was late and the dark would come quickly.

I remembered the words to the Gustav Mahler song, 'Dark is life, is death.' I remembered the words that came after, 'The lovely earth everywhere blossoms in the spring and becomes green again.'

As if in a dream I saw Jason stand and go to the piano. Everything seemed normal. Everything seemed possible.

I was no longer worried about Jason missing a note or forgetting a line. None of that mattered. Dark is life, is death. That is all we know and all we need to know.

Maybe because I was not nervous, Jason was not nervous. Or because he was not nervous, I was not nervous. There was no way to tell the difference.

He played with an insight he had never shown before, translating dynamic markings into something very close to music, sometimes music. There was feeling, there was a sense of an individual interpretation.

At the close I shouted what was supposed to be *bravo* but came out sounding like *ba.* When the woman in the white turtleneck turned around to tell me what she thought of such a half-hearted effort, I went right on clapping and cheering and did not look at her or give her any reason to feel satisfied.

December 14 / Another Word for the Devil

The road home was deep with snow. The harbour, which in places was no more than a stone's throw from the road, remained invisible in the late afternoon squall. It was Saturday. There was no hurry.

At a service station at the edge of town Jason and I stopped to buy a Christmas tree. A man was selling Christmas trees out of a lean-to, with a second-hand Franklin stove on half-broken legs in the dirt that gave out more smoke than fire.

In his long, tattered coat, with his thin, white hair flying in the wind, he reminded me of Robert Frost on the day of his reading at Kennedy's inauguration.

He loved the snow, he said, because it made it feel more like Christmas.

It's good for business too, he admitted. Something in the tone of his voice made it clear that he know the difference between the two.

Jason wanted a tree ten feet high, minimum. With some effort I was able to beat him down to seven.

The old man who looked like Robert Frost found a piece of clothesline to tie down the trunk door. He shook my hand and pumped Jason's. Very best, he said.

He watched us get back on the road and set off, guarding the lane to make sure no cars came along the highway in the heavy snow to plough into the back of us.

The drive up the hill to Crystal Cliffs was difficult in the dark. Twice I was sure I was heading into a ditch.

We can die just as easily as you, I thought. Probably, though, it would not be that easy, or straightforward. It would be messy and bloody.

Everything came easy to you, even dying.

Emma was playing outside, in front of a neighbour's house, when we arrived home. I wanted her to come in, but she refused. She and her friend were having too much fun, putting the finishing touches to a snowman they had built.

The blunt end of a large carrot served for a penis.

You're not supposed to look, Emma said.

You agreed to make the dough for the pizza, I said.

I've already done that.

Be that as it may I want you to come in.

A little longer, please.

Ten minutes, max.

In the kitchen Jason rubbed safflower oil on a cookie sheet and pressed out the dough for the pizza while I rummaged in the fridge for the ingredients for a salad – Romaine lettuce, Belgian endive, Spanish onion, whitecap mushrooms, hothouse tomatoes, cheddar cheese, cashew splits.

In a black iron frying pan Jason sizzled half a pound of bacon to add to his side of the pizza while I washed, cut, and mixed my part of the deal.

Coming in a few minutes earlier than promised, Emma ran up the stairs to the bathroom, leaving in her wake a trail of melting, vanishing-white snow.

I moved to the cutting board close to the stove so that I was standing right next to Jason while he continued tossing and stirring the slices of bacon. I could feel the splash of the grease on my arm.

Something has happened I think you should know about, I said.

Did something happen to Mom?

No, it's not about her.

What then?

Do you remember the man who visited us a couple months ago and came to dinner a couple times?

The monk?

His name was Thomas Merton.

He beat me at backgammon the first time we played, but I won the next game.

He died a few days ago, in some freak accident

in Bangkok.

Where's Bangkok?

In Asia.

Did somebody kill him?

Why do you say that?

I don't know.

Maybe you're right. He was very outspoken. He was against the war. He said America was turning into a fascist country. He talked about going to North Vietnam and giving himself up as a 'hostage to peace.' He took on some powerful forces. I would even call them demonic.

What does *demonic* mean?

Demonic means it has to do with the devil, or with an evil being. Another word for the devil is Satan. Satan is the great enemy of God.

If God made the world, did he make Satan too?

Good question. Let's get the pizza in the oven, and I'll try to give you an answer.

I set the timer at twelve minutes, then opened a bottle of wine and poured a glass for myself. Jason lugged a bottle of Pepsi to the table just inside the glass sliding doors that opened onto the back porch.

We sat facing each other. He looked past me onto the porch while I rambled. As to who made Satan there are at least two views on that. The Christian view is that God created the world and everything in it, including Satan. Satan is a kind of rebel who gets temporarily out of control. The rebellion takes place post creation. Christ comes to subdue the enemy Satan and restore the Kingdom of God. In modern terms, every one of us has the power, with the help of whatever divinity we believe in, to subdue the devil within us.

I sipped my wine. Maybe wine is my divinity, or what wine does to me, I thought. All I know is it works. The other view is called Gnosticism, the idea here is that a lot of things happen before the creation of the world. Some think that Satan rebels and sets himself up in opposition to God. Satan becomes a kind of shadow or half God in his own eyes. Others think that Satan is a power equal to God from the beginning. Equal but opposite. A power for evil and darkness.

In any case it is Satan, not the most-high God, who creates this world that we live in. The most-high God would never create such a world, in all its ugliness. He is not a material God, but a God of pure light. We poor humans get sucked into this world of flesh and blood and forget the other world where the God of light rules. This world is a kind of prison. Jesus comes down from heaven to give us the knowledge we need to get out of prison. The keys to the garden.

Why do they say the world is a kind of prison,

Jason asked. A prison is when you're locked up inside and can't get out.

They say we're locked up in our bodies.

If I didn't have a body, I wouldn't be anybody.

I agree with you completely. So does Christianity. Having a body is very important in the Christian religion. Jesus had a body and it was real. Don't forget, Jesus was a Jew, and for the Jew the body is created in the image of God.

If I didn't have a body, I wouldn't even know I was alive.

My opinion exactly, I assure you. On the other hand Paul has some pretty negative things to say about the body. For example, he says that flesh and blood will never inherit heaven. In general, things of the body are negative, things of the spirit positive. Paul is not a Gnostic, but he comes close. For example, he says at one point, I think it's in the third chapter of Galatians, that the Jewish law is not given by God but by what he calls the *subordinate angel-powers*.

What does *subordinate* mean?

It means having a lower rank.

Jason tilted his head back, lifted the bottle of Pepsi to his lips, and lapped loudly at the last bit of black liquid. I don't even know what you're talking about, he said.

I was trying to answer your question about who made Satan.

You gave me about six different answers. I don't know which one to believe.

Which one you believe is completely up to you.

You never told me what you think.

It doesn't matter what I think. What matters is what you think.

Emma came into the room, her face still a rosy red from playing in the snow.

Think about what, she said.

None of your business, Jason said.

We were talking about evil, I said. What it is, and where it comes from.

Looks like evil just walked in the door, Jason said.

Who cares what you think, Emma said.

I'll get the pizza going, I said. If you two feel like fighting about something, go right ahead. I'll ask the dog to come and referee.

I'm coming with you.

Me too.

If we can all just calm down a little, I think supper's probably ready.

I'm calm.

Me too.

That leaves me.

December 14 / Emma's Dream

The stand for the Christmas tree was in the basement, but I had no idea where in the basement. That sort of thing had been *her* department.

When she vanished she took with her much of the knowledge that I needed in order to keep things up and running. I did want to keep things up and running, I kept telling myself, even when I did not really believe it.

While in town earlier I could have bought a new stand, on sale at half price. Half the price of what I had wondered.

While I rummaged through the many damp and smelly cardboard boxes that were stacked under the basement stairs, the children between them carried the new tree from the garage through the front door of the house, into the hallway. I heard a thud, as someone dropped her end to the floor just above my head.

In a low voice Jason spoke a few unkind words to his sister.

Emma said nothing, only scowled, as I knew only Emma could scowl.

The tree made a noise like fingernails scratching freshly painted drywall as it was dragged down the hall into the living room without ceremony.

At the bottom of a box containing, among other things, a miniature manger, various stuffed animals, a shepherd, three wise men, a piece of gold foil that can be taken to represent the angel Gabriel, and four stockings, each as red and fluffy as cotton candy, to hang by the defunct and boarded-up chimney, I found what I was looking for. The red, chipped rings of metal could hold a thick-enough trunk. The curved steel pieces that were intended to serve as legs for the stand looked more like the pegs for a six-person tent.

At seven feet tall the tree scraped the ceiling, leaving no room for the twisted, pathetic angel. Just as well, I sighed, casting the foil aside, onto the carpet beneath the piano bench.

Emma looked at me in wonder and astonishment, but said nothing. It had been a long time since she had seen me this carefree. The living room itself had not seen this much activity since the previous Christmas, with the possible exception of the odd sleep-over when Emma had gone out of her way to prove that she was not the eternal loner but did indeed have a friend or two.

The limbs of the tree, in the warmth of the room, fluffed out like the tail of a pheasant standing its ground and honking.

I went first, stringing the tree with lights, beginning at the bottom and working up, in this way making my way somewhat tediously from front to back and around again.

Jason arranged bulbs and ornaments, some of glass, some of cloth, some baked hard and fast. Emma sprinkled tinsel over everything, like tears over a multitude of sins.

The news of your death had touched something deep and almost forgotten in everyone's heart. We were walking on eggshells.

Emma, having completed her task, gave me a brief, sharp glance, as if to say, there, I've done what you wanted me to do, now leave me alone. It was a look of disapproval and hurt, much like the look Jason had given me at the end of our long and confusing talk just concluded.

Do I no longer know how to talk to my own children, I asked myself. Am I losing my way here on these grounds where I should be most at home?

The tree occupied one corner of the room. I sat on the couch and watched Jason hang ornaments and Emma sprinkle tinsel, everyone now glum as a ski lodge in a downpour of rain.

On the glass coffee table was a stack of art and photography books as big as folios, a jar of peppermint candies, a glass ashtray shaped like a owl, a box of stick matches, two tall, brass candle holders that used to belong to her, before we met.

I struck a match and lit the candles. I closed my eyes and tried to remember what it was like when we first met. When I opened my eyes again, Emma was sitting on the couch next to me. Jason had gone from the room and was nowhere to be seen.

I felt a heavy weight fall from my shoulders, as it became clear that Emma did not despise me – did not see me as the cause of all her present woes.

I had a dream about Mom she said.

Do you want to tell me about it?

That man, Thomas Merton, was in it too.

That's all right, go ahead, I don't mind.

I was in Mom's bookstore. I was showing her my math homework. It was all about factoring. I hate factoring. I said I couldn't do it. He came in but he looked different. He looked Chinese, wearing an orange robe, with a belt made of some kind of rope, like the kind they use on boats. The belt was purple.

He said something to Mom. It was like I wasn't there. He told her how he had died. He said it was not suicide like some people were saying. 'I touched a live wire on purpose because I had a wish to join the Infinite,' he said. 'Tell me what it's like, the Infinite,'

Mom said. 'I spent too much time looking in the wrong place,' he said. Then he left. On the way out he saw me for the first time. He bowed to me, like I was a king or something.

I think he was bowing to the child in you.

Mom followed him and I went outside out to find them. But then I woke up.

You probably didn't want to know.

Do you think he's still alive and living in another body?

No, I don't believe that.

Is Mom still alive?

I like to believe she is.

I wish she'd call.

Jason came back into the room, with a tray on which he had placed three bowls of vanilla ice cream. He put the tray down on the coffee table, took one bowl for himself, and found a place to sit on the piano bench.

Emma went next, then me.

I don't know how to say this, I said. The thing is, it wasn't his fault. She left without telling us why, but that was her choice. We can't blame him.

He wasn't like other people.

It was like he was living in another world.

Maybe it was an accident that killed him, because he wasn't paying attention.

What does *accident* mean?

It means it wasn't planned.

In the dream he said he planned it himself.

What dream?

None of your business.

I suppose you think you're psychic.

What if I am? It's better than being a klutz like you.

I suppose you can tell the future.

Maybe I can.

If you're so smart, tell me what you see right now.

I see you in the year nineteen hundred ninety-two. I hate to tell you this, but you're still a klutz.

You see, you don't know anything. You just like to pretend.

If you would shut up for a minute, maybe I could concentrate.

Wow, *concentrate*. I'm surprised you can even say the word, with an IQ like yours.

Hush now, you two. Jason, let her be.

Stung, Jason leaned into his bowl of ice cream, while Emma, breathing easier, sat up on the edge of the couch, her back straight, her head tipped forward, her eyes closed.

They were so different, yet so alike. The same

colour skin, the same thick, dark hair. The same intensely inward gaze.

Without opening her eyes Emma said, I see the clock on the table by my bed. It says five o'clock. I can see it because the moon is shining in the window. It's Christmas morning. I can tell it's Christmas morning because everything is so quiet. I get up from bed and look in Jason's room but he's still sleeping. I look in Dad's room but he's snoring. I go downstairs. The glass of brandy we left on the table is gone. It's dark, but I can see everything. I can see the angel Gabriel on top of the tree.

Before I even look around, I know Mom is there. She's sitting on the piano bench, where Jason is now. She's holding the glass of brandy in one hand and the other hand is on the edge of the bench. She smiles at me.

Emi, honey, for your sake, for all our sakes, I hope it's true.

I was never wrong before.

I know, I know.

Two Years Later / Banks of Dark Mud

I did not read the first week. I walked in the woods, or waited by the river for the tide to come in.

Sometimes I did better than this. There were times when the October sun warmed a bed for me in the tall grass in front of my cabin, on the hill above the river.

Hidden in the grass, away from the path behind the cabin that others on retreat might use, I lay undisturbed, forgetful of time.

Birds sang, sometimes very near, sometimes far off. Or they flittered through the grass like crisp leaves.

I was part of the earth, yet light as their song.

I did not mind how the hours went by.

Instead of singing like the birds, I stayed quite still, listening to everything that was happening around me – listening to the silence.

For an hour before the tide came in the mud banks smelled of almonds.

I went into the woods, pounding down the trail as hard as any black bear to the beach below. Pounding my chest and chanting *almond smell, almond smell.*

It was the way the sun baked the salt and the other deposits on the soft mounds of mud in the long interval between high and low tides that gave rise to the peculiar smell.

When the tide came in, it carried with it the smell of ferns though this was fleeting and difficult to catch.

On foggy days it smelled of printer's ink.

I wondered where these extra smells came from, whether from inside me or from outside. There was a correspondence that struck me as auspicious.

I was always hungry and could not sleep more than five hours. I waited on the side of the hill to see the first car on the highway across the river.

Sometimes I waited an hour but I did not mind.

I imagined a man with a factory job, or a doctor who worked shifts in emergency.

I imagined a man with a wife and children. Did the wife get up to see him off? Did the children? Did he like the job he was going to?

I imagined meeting this same man on a downtown street. We would be strangers, with very different lives, yet we would share this experience of rising before dawn.

We would feel bound by it, even if we could not name what it was we shared.

I followed the cars as they moved along the road above the mud banks. They seemed so close across the deep tidal river that I was surprised that I could not hear them.

They moved along noiselessly, ghost-like. Motion was the only reality. All else was shadow and play.

In the water below the highway a blue heron came to feed early every morning. Some mornings it was there before I was.

In the dark it was a presence that brought life to wide stretches of the black, icy water.

When the first car came down the road out of the woods, the great bird rose into the air and flew across the river, with a slow and clumsy show of wings.

A protected marsh a hundred yards upriver from the retreat where I was staying was its destination. It settled there in the tall grasses.

The retreat stressed quiet and meditation. Everyone stayed in separate cabins, without exception. Close friends, lovers, husbands and wives all took cabins far removed from each other.

The sixty acres of woodland on the rolling hills above the river, hiding twenty primitive cabins, made it easy to go for days without meeting another soul. The rule was a simple one – avoid eye contact, talk to no one.

Every evening the director of the retreat gave a talk. Sometimes he posed a series of questions that he took delight in leaving unanswered.

The only wisdom he claimed was the wisdom of experience. For some this evening talk was an eagerly awaited event, a chance to be among fellow human beings, though again the idea was to listen, not mix and mingle.

For others, like myself, it was an event that I was happy to miss, to forget, to skip, to avoid, to strike from the list of things to do.

My cabin was far from the main building, in the woods above a creek that flowed into the river. I lived at the margin of the retreat and at the margin of life.

If I was looking for anything it was for the truth about the nature of life when it is lived at the margin.

After breakfast I sat in a wooden lawn chair on the hill and watched the currents on the surface of the water shifting and changing. At times the currents flowed straight and steady. At times they curved, twisted, and skirted invisible barriers.

The steady, powerful, invisible currents when the tide was going out seemed, to my mind, like the currents in a man's or a woman's soul – always there, always tugging, always shaping and reshaping the contours of life.

The soul feels a strong downward pull toward a world of darkness and emptiness, which it fights against at its own peril.

Toward town the river narrowed. The water had a delicate shade of pink to it. The hills, with the water flowing through them, were pre-historic, idle, mysterious.

I was able to see everything up close. I had the ability to go out into things.

Fasting was a way to see into the heart of things. Some days I ate nothing till evening. Some days I ate nothing at all.

Normal fare was minimal. Breakfast might consist of a piece of bread washed down with a cup of instant coffee. Lunch was a bag of nuts and raisins, together with a piece of cheddar cheese.

I ate one apple a day, at four o'clock, sitting on a favourite log and looking across the rock-strewn beach. Supper was a peanut butter and grape jelly sandwich, followed by an assortment of raw vegetables.

I kept instant coffee, herbal tea, nuts, raisins, and other non-perishables in the cabin. Perishables were placed in a plastic-lined hole in the ground next to the cabin.

Those supplicants staying for long periods could expect to find some meat once a week, usually dried fish. On special occasions there was a spicy beef stew that could be warmed on the wood stove.

A few minutes before the tide came in the birds along the river, sensing what was in the offing, flew up in a circling, squawking, disorderly chorus of welcome.

Ducks took flight up river, keeping low over the water until they disappeared from sight.

Sandpipers swooped near the shoreline, in perfect formation, before settling in the safer grounds of the marsh above the mud banks.

These were the common birds. More uncommon was the family of bald eagles that nested in the woods across the river from the retreat.

The sight of these birds – a male and a female – surprised me toward the end of my first week.

It was a Friday. The tide was out. The sun was low in the sky. Already there was a chill in the air.

I had been pacing the rock-strewn beach, above the crusted mud banks, gazing down river, chanting *almond smell, almond smell.* The first thing I noticed was a movement above the river, something that was there that had not been there previously.

It could have been anything – a cloud, a plane, or a shadow thrown across the sky. But before I looked I knew it was something alive, animate.

It circled near, in search of food, the white head and white rump plainly visible.

The circling had something methodical,

mechanical in it that was menacing.

A moment later, as if by accident, the bird caught an air current and rode it skyward. It became a small black dot high above.

The second bird – the female – repeated the same pattern. Then, in the blink of an eye, both were gone.

For several days there was heavy rain, and the creek became swollen with run-off.

The day the rain stopped was a warm, misty, grey day.

The sun made an appearance late in the afternoon. It was not much more than a glow in the middle of a thinning cloud cover.

I waded through the wet grass and down the side of the hill to the water. Vapour rose around me, out of the press of the hills.

I sprinkled my face with water. The blue jay on the limb of the white birch tree, surprised by my presence, lifted off in protest.

I slipped naked into the rush of the creek, the orifices of my body closing against the coldness. I went out from the shore and caught the flow of the water rushing down the hills into the river.

I let it carry me down, to a place where I could hold a birch branch. I swung around on my belly and felt the current.

The water let me down again and it broke against my nose. The current was strong against my hips, pushing them out.

I let go of every thought, every desire, every need, except the need to hold tight to the birch branch.

The Second Week / You Belong to Me Now

At the beginning of the second week I began to
read again.

For an hour in the evening, while the light was
available, I sat outside my cabin in a lawn chair where I
could see below to the creek where it flowed into the
river.

The murmuring of the creek was background to
the reading I was doing.

Sometimes I dozed in the warm sun. I could
lose myself in the sounds the water made or in the
singing of the birds all around me, in the trees and on the
ground.

I existed outside my body, just as much as
inside. I felt as light as the warm air.

What was amazing was that I had nothing to do.
No one wanted me. No one was calling for me. No one
missed me.

All around me the birds sang. Little chickadees
darted down to pick a dinner out of my woodpile, calling
out a lively *day day day.*

One of them alighted on the flat piece of wood
where my arm rested and pecked away without fear.

The hairs on the back of my arm were the colour of burnished gold.

I wondered if they were mine, or someone else's, whom I had never met.

Another bird alighted on my shoulder while I sat in the lawn chair. I felt more thrilled while the creature remained than by any medals I could have worn.

The deep, angry croak of a raven woke me from my daydream.

I went along a hilltop path toward the place where the creek emptied into the river. A pine tree was growing at an angle into the side of the hill.

A lone raven flew off from the tangle of limbs as I approached.

Just beyond the pine tree I looked down on a scene of strife and contention, as a bald eagle, having already flushed a number of ravens from a food pile, was attempting to tear away some of its prize.

Two of the ravens stood near the eagle, while a third struck out, biting and pulling the eagle's tail. The eagle turned giving the other two a chance to get in behind and steal a bite.

When the eagle saw this it chased one of the fleeing ravens allowing the others to converge on the food pile, reclaiming it as their own.

Later, when I went down to the beach to look at

what remained of the carcass, I saw bones and raw flesh, with guts exposed.

From the size of the bones I guessed it was a deer. It had come far, to be here. Far from the protection of the woods.

Possibly it had drowned in the recent flood and been washed out. Possibly a hunter had shot wide of the mark, inflicting a wound, before turning and walking away.

It had come far in its confusion. The ravens had eaten well. It was nature's way.

I stepped lightly, on ground that felt sacred, this close to this much carnage.

Death was the great letting go. The peace that comes over the dead like a blessing is the peace of letting go. There is nothing greater than this.

Too often the killer does not know this side of the story. The killer remains ignorant and therefore arrogant.

The woods between the cabin and the river were exposed to the fierce, salt-laden wind that blew in from the bay of the ocean ten miles away.

In these woods the trees were in every stage of decay.

By the river there was a row of spruce trees completely stripped of bark and limbs, one tilted at such an angle, across the others, that I expected to see it come crashing down at any moment.

Closer to the cabin, in a riot of ferns and raspberry bushes, was a rotting tree trunk, fifteen feet high, broken straight across by the wind, inside which, one morning, I heard the scratching of an animal.

I stopped where I was, stood quietly by, and waited for the animal to appear. Waited an hour and more without moving.

Finally the scratching stopped. I walked around the tree, circling closer, but still four or five feet away.

On the north side of the tree, at a height of between seven and eight feet, was a hole big enough for a bird to get in and out. The hole was empty. No sound came from inside the tree.

I moved back, where the woods were thicker, where I could still see the hole but from a safe distance. I waited another twenty minutes.

A bird emerged and darted away so quickly that I could only note the manner of flight – a deeply undulating movement, produced by several rapid beats of the wings followed by a pause, and the flash of a broad, white rump.

A second bird appeared almost immediately, but flew only a short distance to the branch of a nearby tree, perhaps to await a signal from its partner.

It had chosen a tree where the sun shone brightly, and I could see the bird in full glory.

The brown wings had dozens of attractive, black-rimmed, white spots.

The side of the breast was a rich camel colour.

At the top of the breast was a wide, pure-black crescent.

On the cheek, below the eye, a smaller black mark.

The long bill gave the head a strong, balanced shape.

As the bird turned its head, I caught a glimpse of a red patch on the nape.

With this turning I heard a short burst of its song, a loud but pleasant *wick wick wick*.

It was the same song I had been hearing for days in different parts of the woods.

Then this second bird disappeared into deeper woods.

As I walked back to my cabin, I sang to myself,

> *I have seen you beauty.*
> *You belong to me now,*
> *Whoever you were waiting for.*
> *If I never see you again*
> *You belong to me*
> *And these woods belong to me*

The last week of the retreat was a week of cloud and rain.

The second to last day it rained heavily and the creek flooded again but this time with water much too cold for swimming.

On the last day the clouds broke at mid-morning, and the sun came out.

I celebrated the return of the sun and the end of the retreat by preparing a picnic on the hill above the river.

A little distance from the pine tree where I had first seen the neighbourhood ravens, on the softest grass I could find, I spread a blanket and arranged small plates of cheddar cheese, oatmeal bread, sultana raisins, mixed nuts, slices of a red apple, and a jug of cold water from the spring in the woods beside the director's cabin.

I had had nothing to eat since the previous evening. I was hungry.

Here's to you, Woodpecker. I raised my glass high.

And here's to you, Raven.

And to you, Eagle.

And to you, Director of Retreats. There's none better.

I was drunk, not with wine but with possibilities.

A few hundred yards along the beach, below the property adjacent to the retreat, where the river grew wide before emptying into the bay, I spotted a man and a boy gathering sun-blackened seaweed for mulch.

The man had on yellow rubber boots and green gardening gloves to work the slick, muddy beach. The boy did his best to hold open the large orange garbage bags into which the man dumped armload after armload of seaweed.

Seeing them work together, seeing how their movements flowed and interweaved so easily, hearing the occasional muted word spoken, I felt alone for the first time since coming on retreat.

I remembered Jason, far away at university, so silent.

I remembered Emma, already a mother at sixteen, with all the worries and burdens that I could do nothing to ease.

Tears are a blessing, no matter what brings them on.

No matter what comes after.

Something sharp breaks the ice inside.

The waters flow.

The pink on the surface was turning to grey.

The silence was so complete that I could hear

the gurgling of the water where the tide was beginning to turn.

There was a sense of release, but from what I did not know.

I cried, knowing all the time that someone was standing next to me, not talking, but feeling the same thing.

I sensed something at my back. I turned to look.

Within ten feet of me, following the course of the creek down to the river, no higher than the tops of the trees, a bald eagle glided by.

Frozen in place by the hugeness and the strangeness of it, I watched without moving.

The bird continued on, then dropped like a dead weight below the lip of the hill, out of sight.

Real or imagined, it did not matter.

I ran along the top of the hill, looking, looking, until I came to the edge of the cliff above the beach in time to see the bird fly out over the water.

It caught an air current and rode it skyward, as it had done countless times before.

Great bird, graceful in flight, merciless in attack, I murmured to myself, echoing the murmur of the creek that I had heard for weeks without understanding.

Come back, I called. And found myself laughing at the foolishness of it.

Acknowledgements

The books by Thomas Merton that I have drawn most heavily from are *The Sign of Jonas, Conjectures of a Guilty By-Stander, The Alaskan Journals,* and *The Seven Storey Mountain.* I also acknowledge the debt I owe to Michael Mott's biography, *The Seven Mountains of Thomas Merton,* especially for the information it gives regarding the last few months of Merton's life.

About the Author

Edward Lemond was born in Lafayette, Indiana and came to Canada in 1969. He lived in Halifax, Nova Scotia for 24 years before moving to his present home, in Moncton, New Brunswick. He owned and operated the Attic Owl Bookshop, a second-hand and antiquarian bookstore, for 21 years before retiring in 2008. He is a founding organizer of the Northrop Frye Literary Festival, held annually in Moncton. He has published stories in *Quarry, The Antigonish Review,* and *Galleon.* Several of his poems have appeared in *The Antigonish Review.* His poetry collection is called *Overheard. Birds of Appetite* was short-listed for the 2011 Ken Klonsky Novella Contest.